NOT THAT BRUCE WILLIS!

A STORY OF REDEMPTION

PAMELA HOFFMAN

ILLUSTRATED BY:

HOLLY LEANNE HAMLIN-HOFFMAN

REDEEMED_SAVED2 PUBLISHING

OKLAHOMA

Not That Bruce Willis!

A Story of Redemption

Redeemed_Saved2 books may be ordered through booksellers Amazon, Barnes Noble, ect.

http//www.pamelajeanhoffman.com

ISBN: 13:978-0692349113

ISBN:-10:0692349111

Library of Congress Control Number: 2011905024

Publication dates: iUniverse date: 4/18/2011

Redeemed_Saved2 date: 3/25/2015

Contents

Chapter 1 - Uninvited Guests.. 7

Chapter 2 - Not That Bruce Willis.. 13

Chapter 3 - The Escape 23

Interlude 27

Chapter 4 - Hope 31

Interlude 34

Chapter 5 - Ready? Action! 35

Interlude 42

Chapter 6 - The Unbelievable 43

Interlude 50

Chapter 7 - Visions 53

Interlude 59

Chapter 8 - Friends or Enemies 61

Interlude 69

Chapter 9 - Mrs. Felder 71

Interlude 75

Chapter 10 - Waiting... 77

Interlude 81

Chapter 11 - Martha.. 83

Interlude 90

Chapter 12 - Revelations... 91

Interlude 99

Chapter 13 - Peace 101

Epilogue 105

A Note from the Author.. 107

Enjoy this excerpt from: Falcon Feather; A Story of Salvation........ 109

Chapter 1 - Uninvited Guests

"Chesterfield, let's finish this last calf. Don't let that snot-nosed heifer outmaneuver you! Cut her off, boy! That's it. Hold her steady now."

Chesterfield shakes his mane and holds the rope tight as I bail off, following it all the way to the sick calf. She doesn't give me much of a fight, thank goodness. I just don't think I have another fight left in me after a long day of riding and doctoring contrary calves. Flipping her on her side, I give her a shot of penicillin and let her up. Taking the lariat off of her neck, I turn, smiling because we are finally finished. Her momma charges head-on and head-butts me over the calf's back. Landing on my back, I slide through the manure that the heifer has just deposited everywhere. After the wind is knocked out of me, it takes a little while to get my wits about me. The baked ground feels like cement; my aching body feels like it has been thrown up against a concrete wall. I realize I'm under the belly of one of the cows; I'm staring right up at her udder. Her calf looks at me and bellers, "Maaaaaaaaaa," as if to say,

"Mine!" I scramble out of there just as the cow kicks. I grab my hat and my horse's reins. Swinging into the saddle, Chesterfield and I head home just as the sun is going down. We started our day before the sun came up, and we will finish just as it sinks out of sight.

Our day started with the Texas Panhandle sun casting a lustrous hue over the sky. I rode for an hour before the sun began to peek over the edge of the plateaus. As the first rays fell, the cap rock seemed aglow. The crystals within glistened in the sun. The red clay gave striking contrast to the grayish-white dusted sage, weeds, grasses, and small scrub cedars. The plateaus appeared as unique tabletops; it seemed as if a tablecloth lay upon the land. The heavy folds lay in shadows of red as they created deep ravines ending in voluminous canyons. I realized how much I love this land. I love the Canadian River Valley and Wolf Creek areas.

Chesterfield and I have taken all day checking the various water holes. We've made sure the cattle have plenty to drink. The hot summer has taken its toll on the grass pastures and the water supply. The spring that runs across the back of the property and feeds into Wolf Creek is barely trickling. This tells me that Ogallala Aquifer is getting low. The small creeks it feeds are all but dried up. The windmills tapped into the aquifer are in good shape, but if the wind didn't blow for a couple of days in a row we would have to be hauling water to the cattle. In response to my thoughts, a hot summer's breeze blows against my face once more. My sweat-stained shirt feels cooler, even though the breeze is warm. Looking to the west, it seems to be getting dark early. There is a huge, dark bank of clouds forming in the southwest. They blot out the retreating sun's glow.

I ask God to let the plants and animals have some fresh water. I have only just begun to whisper small prayers to God again. I'm so unworthy, I can't possibly ask for anything for myself, or boldly speak to God aloud. I abandoned God for three years to pursue my own selfish desires. I know with all of my heart that it was my own abandonment and not God's. God is constant. He doesn't move from us. We must consciously make the choice to walk away from Him and His blessings. I've come a long way to own my mistakes and accept responsibility for my choices. I knew after mom's death that I needed to man up and be the man she saw in me.

We arrive at the ranch with both of our stomachs growling. Or maybe it's just mine. I swing my manure-laden leg over Chesterfield's rump. My foot hits the ground, and my leg almost buckles under. I have chased down several ornery, sick calves and given them a shot of penicillin today. In all of the commotion, I've slipped and fallen more times than I care to remember. Every bone in my body aches, especially my tailbone.

"Chesterfield, why do calves have to get diarrhea every time they get sick?" I ask the tall, ghostly-white bay. I don't expect an answer, but Chesterfield always responds. This time it's a toss of his head back and forth, as if to say, *I don't know.* The southwesterly breeze lifts more of the powdery, grayish-white dust from Chesterfield and me, creating swirling apparitions of undefined figures.

I hobble toward the barn with Chesterfield. I feel much older than my twenty years. In the last three years I have seen betrayal, loneliness, addiction, rejection, and the death of my mother. I loved her so very much that I still don't know how to deal with life without her. The previous three years have left me weary and worn. I can trace most of my pain back to the love of one girl—the only girl for me, I used to think. I know all too well that people can idolize things on this earth. I did that with Cindy. She was the most important thing to me. I abandoned everything I was taught to be with her. I left God and His love. I ignored my parent's wishes, when all they wanted was what was best for me. I remember the Ten Commandments that I memorized years ago. One in particular stands out from the others.

"You shall have no other gods before me" (Ex. 20:3).

I know I worshipped Cindy. She became the most important thing in my life, to the exclusion of everything else. I know prayer is a personal conversation with my God. Someone talks and someone listens, as in any conversation. Trouble is, I talked but failed to listen. When I took the time to still my mind, I'd hear what God wanted me to know and I always felt blessed. In my heart of hearts I know that I'm unworthy of such intimacy. I can't believe that I chose Cindy and her lifestyle over my Lord. Mom always saw me as a man following God. I never knew why, because I was off that path more than on it for years.

I have to clear my mind and stay in the present. Dwelling on the past consumes me with grief. It weakens me and tempts me to blot out the pain with alcohol or drugs. I have to heal and get my life back. I have to be strong.

I want to see Mom again in heaven and be able to hold my head high. I will become the man she saw in me!

Inhaling deeply, clearing my mind, I focus on the familiar smells around me. I love the smell of the fresh, sweet grass hay that is stored in the loft of the barn for the winter. It reminds me of endless summer days and playing in the hay. I never have a worry in the world when I'm lying in the hay.

After our ride, Chesterfield and I look more like ghosts than anything else. I smile, thinking of the legends of ghostly Indians traveling the land. The light wind kicks up the powder, coating us. In the twilight, I can see how someone might mistake a person for a ghost. Looking now across the prairie in the waning light, I watch as the dust dances to a tune only it hears.

Gazing out over the land, I think of how rich it is in the history of this country. So many people have passed this way, prehistoric dwellers having lived along Wolf Creek. They left behind the crude structures they called home, but only the foundations remain now. Many Native Americans have traveled through the area. There is even a cave on the Willis property that has some pictures drawn by those travelers, showing that they hunted antelope and buffalo. The drawings also show a river running through the land. I guess that would be Wolf Creek or maybe the Canadian River. It would have been important to know where you could get water and food. Even Coronado ventured into my world. He came this far north in search of the legendary City of Gold.

I unsaddle Chesterfield affectionately and wash him down, brushing him as I let the water run over that beautiful red coat. I wash the white dust from his black mane and tail. I feel each black-socked leg, lifting it to make sure the shoes are in good shape.

I turn off the water and set Chesterfield loose in the meadow behind the barn. He immediately runs to the piece of ground barren of grass and lies down. He rolls over and over, scratching his back. He twitches his rump from side to side, swinging his long neck and head toward his rump as he lies in the dirt. Shaking my head, I call out to my companion, "I don't know why I bother with you. Your next bath can be when it rains!"

After saying this, I glance once more at the clouds. They are darker and closer; perhaps we will get a rain. I hang the tack and saddle in the barn. I think I hear the rumble of thunder as static charges flash across the sky in the distance. Chesterfield gives a snort and a whinny and jumps to his feet. He perks his ears straight up and turns them toward the driveway. I follow my friend's attentive gaze. There is a black SUV coming down the drive. Perhaps that is what he has heard. Whoever it is will be here within ten to fifteen minutes, even with stopping to open the gates in the pasture.

I sprint to the back of the house and shuck my clothes. I grab the rank, manure-coated jeans and grimy, sweaty shirt and put them in the hamper. I change my mind too late on where they should go. They should stay outside instead of dumping them inside the house. Now the adjacent indoor bathroom will reek.

There is an outdoor shower that has exterior access doors. I can access a cabinet and the hamper from either the outdoor shower or the bathroom in the house. I step under the shower head and vigorously wash my long hair. I need a haircut, but I hate going to town. There are just too many temptations. I wash the rest of my body. I ache so much, it would have been wonderful to just stand under the warm water and let the tension of the day drain away with the water. I reach into the cabinet where clean clothes are kept. I haven't used the outdoor shower for a few summers, and from the looks of the clothes stored in the cupboard, I haven't used it since I was fifteen.

I hear the car come to a stop in the front yard and notice that the outdoor lights on the house and grounds have turned on due to the darkness. I don't have a choice, so I throw on the gray sweatpants. The elastic at the bottoms of the legs hits me mid-calf. I try pulling the pants way down on my bony hips, barely covering my butt—if I had one. The T-shirt I find is from a Scout camp I attended when I was fifteen. I pull it on and it fits like my own skin, except that it stops two inches short of my belly button. The short sleeves disappear somewhere around my armpits, making the short-sleeved shirt look like a muscle shirt. Glancing at the reflective stainless steel wall of the shower, I see a sight so comical it's scary. My hair is bushed out about three inches, traveling every which way in the breeze. My tiny, brown muscle shirt has a large, bright-yellow arrowhead on the front.

The doorbell rings. The low-slung pants do nothing for me. I pull them up and they look like long shorts. At least now the shirt almost touches the top of my pants. The doorbell rings again, longer this time. I smooth my wild hair as I race through the house to the front door.

"Just a minute; I'm coming."

I frantically look around for shoes. I open the coat closet by the door, and there is a pair of flip-flops with a palm tree on the thingy that goes between my toes. They were once a prop for a high school play. Now there is pounding on the door. I have no choice; I step into the flip-flops and swing the door open. I sport my smile with confidence. The smile is supposed to distract my uninvited guests from noticing my appearance.

"Hello, I'm Bruce Willis. Can I help you?" I said politely.

The three men before me make eye contact. Then slowly their eyes travel down all six foot three inches of me to my flip-flops. They linger there for a moment before retracing their gaze back up my body to end at my hair. They are speechless.

Chapter 2 - Not That Bruce Willis

"Not *that* Bruce Willis, of course! My parents liked action movies. You know, like *Die Hard*? Oh, never mind. Can I help you?" I start to explain, but I know it is hopeless. Besides these men don't look like they have a sense of humor.

The shortest man steps forward and puts his hand on the doorknob. The big, bouncer-looking guy in back smiles; perhaps he at least has a sense of humor. By their looks, these men seem to be an unlikely group. The one in front looks "slick" in his expensive dress pants, button-down shirt, and Florsheim's Maloy dress shoes. The one beside him seems out of his element in dress slacks and a pullover knit shirt. His shoes are obviously an old pair but have probably never been worn much. I wonder if this guy is on drugs. He fidgets all the time and can't seem to control his movements, and he has a facial tic, so I watch him carefully. The big bouncer-looking guy seems likable; he looks like a big child that someone else has dressed for the occasion. I am more than aware that the front man has a firm grip on the doorknob, but as yet they haven't told me why they are at my door. I keep a firm grip on the doorknob as well.

"We've come to talk to your father about using our product," says the man with his hand on the door. "It's cattle feed, specially blended for weight enhancement." He smiles only slightly; or is he baring his teeth like an animal sizing up his prey? I wonder. Their smiles are definitely false, except for the one in the back. He truly seems amused; or is he just happy?

I'm getting very good at detecting posers. During those three years I chose to be away from God, I met many posers. I gained some street smarts, but at what price? I trust no one now, not even myself. Those years have left me empty and paranoid. Maybe it's the drugs that have left me paranoid. For whatever reason, something about these men sets off alarms in the back of my mind. I know I should be careful. There isn't a neighbor close enough to hear me call for help, so I respond, "It's kinda late for a business call, isn't it?"

"Your dad and I went to college together," says the first man, smiling slightly again. "He said if I was ever out this way to stop by the ranch. He wanted to hear about our product. We were in the area and thought we would take the chance of catching him at home."

"Well, my dad isn't able to come to the door right now, but I'll go tell him you're here," I reply evasively. "Who may I tell him is calling?" I hope to buy me some time to figure out what I need to do. I definitely don't want them to know I am alone. My dad is in town and probably won't be home tonight—or any other for that matter.

"I'm Mr. Jones, and I'm the one that went to school with your dad. This is Mr. Brown; he takes care of marketing and has our product pamphlets in his briefcase. And last but not least, in the back is Mr. Smith, the brains of this enterprise." The man chuckles as if there is an inside joke that only he and Mr. Brown know anything about, because Mr. Smith beams at the compliment, and I don't get it at all.

My mind races as they talk. My dad hasn't spent five nights at the ranch since mom died of cancer a year ago, and I haven't left the ranch except to get supplies and to talk to my dad at the office.

We own the local feedlot. The office has an efficiency apartment upstairs, and he sleeps there every night. He tries to get me to move to town with him, but I keep refusing. I know if I'm ever to heal, I have to stay clear of people and temptations. My dad, on the other hand, drowns in sorrow when he's at the ranch. All around us are memories—some good ones of family times and some bad ones, like the oil wells that failed to buy my mother's health. The wells represent great wealth, but it's a false security to believe that money can give you anything you desire.

14

My dad wanted to save my mom and protect me. The money failed him. He felt he had failed her. I think he just gave up on saving me. I disappointed him so many times. It was just easier for me to escape the knowledge that my mom was dying. I ignored the cancer altogether.

I immersed myself in Cindy, a girl I had known all my life. In grade school, we were best friends. We traded pictures, notes, and our dreams. I thought we were getting closer all the time until sixth grade.

That year her parents divorced, and they could think only of themselves. Cindy was at the age when she wanted attention. She didn't get it from her parents, so she looked to the world. To be popular, you had to conform to what the "in" crowd wanted you to be, and being a Christian was not popular. You had to be willing to laugh at others, find their faults, and gossip about them, all the while saying it was in the name of a joke. She enjoyed the rowdy crowd, the ones who liked to skip school and live by their own rules. The smaller she made people feel, the bigger she felt about herself. She used and abused those she called friends. I always thought she was trying to cause her parents to get back together to save her from herself. Neither of her parents spent any time with her to help guide her and bring some balance to her way of thinking.

I listened as a good friend and told her that everything she wanted to do was all right. I wish now that I hadn't done that. But my top priority was to get to talk to her. I thought that was what friends were supposed to say. It was hard to hear her say she wanted to date boys much older than us. I found that she dumped her troubles on me and left me high and dry. If I had told her the truth, that what she was doing would ruin her life, I knew she would never speak to me again.

I asked my mother why a girl would act this way, and she said that she didn't know why someone would choose the world over God. As for the question about her interest in older boys, Mom said that girls sometimes matured physically faster than boys. She also pointed out that belittling others was never mature.

I was not ready to trade in my precious relationship with God for the drama of middle school or junior high friendships. Cindy was growing further and further away. She began dating early, when she was about fourteen. Her folks were going through their second divorces, and neither one wanted to be responsible for her. As a result, she was able to come and go as she pleased from about sixth grade through high school.

I found out about my mom's cancer in my junior year. I needed someone to confide my fears to and sought out Cindy. She listened, but she only hung around me as long as my money lasted. Like a mouse being conditioned to respond to stimuli, by my senior year I was the "go to" guy. I made the parties happen. My unlimited amount of money could buy whatever my "friends" wanted. It bought me Cindy—for a while, anyway.

Jarred suddenly from my deep thoughts, I make eye contact with my guests.

I see Mr. Brown's gaze linger on the surveillance camera and the lock on the door. I watch him sizing up the place, and I'm helpless to do anything about it. I'm more than a little edgy now. I know from my couple of years scoring drugs and alcohol for my buddies that these men are not the kind you trust.

I wish I had left the door locked and ignored their knock, but it gets lonely out in the country. I was really kind of glad to see someone.

"Please, sit at the table here on the porch," I tell them. "It's a beautiful evening. I'll go tell my dad you're here."

I'm sure my dad knows a Jones, a Smith, and a Brown from college. I wonder what their real names are and what they really want. *Gee, I think, I need to get a grip. I need to learn to trust people again. They might actually be old friends of Dad's, and my paranoia is taking on a life of its own.* Thinking of Cindy and her betrayal always sets off my paranoia.

Mr. Jones has his hand on the doorknob and holds it tight as I try to close the door. I straighten up to my full height and take in a deep breath to make my chest look as large as my tiny Scout T-shirt will allow. A fleeting thought that the arrowhead might intimidate them crosses my mind, making me smile inwardly. Outwardly, I level my gaze down a few inches to meet Mr. Jones's stare.

16

In the air, I feel the tension of impending danger. I feel this same tension when I'm making a poor choice.

"I said, 'sit at the table out here'!"

Jerking the door out of Mr. Jones's hand, I close it. Then I close the interior door as well. In the security of the hall, I calm down and think that they might be telling the truth. I don't lock the doors, because it might offend them. Although everything in my being is screaming *Danger!* I make myself walk to the back of the house. As soon as they can no longer see me through the windows, I burst into a sprint, grab my cell phone, hit my dad's speed dial number, and begin looking for a weapon in the kitchen drawers. The first drawer has my grandfather's pocket knife.

My hand is on the knife when someone from behind me grabs the phone, ending the call. I pocket the knife as I turn. My quick temper flares now, and I swing, but I'm immediately brought to my knees by Mr. Smith. He yanks me off my feet by my hair, pulling me backwards. I land on my tailbone for about the fifth time today. My head is bent back, and I am lying on the tiled kitchen floor. I am at a definite disadvantage and outnumbered.

Right in my face, Mr. Jones asks, sneering, "Who are you calling, Scout?"

"I said I would tell my dad you were here. He's at work. That was who you wanted to see, right?" I say this just a little too sarcastically because of the "scout" comment. Mr. Smith back-hands me across the face, splitting my bottom lip open. Blood drips onto the tip of the yellow arrowhead.

I have to control my temper and compose myself. I will need to keep my cool if I'm to survive. These men mean trouble. I have seen men like these before.

I remember the time I was to go after some drugs for a party Cindy was having. My friend hopped in with me at the last minute. He met with the dealers. I had sprained my foot in basketball and couldn't walk very well. We were faced with the same kind of men. There was a difference,

17

though. I was the one sent to make the deal, but I had stayed in the car. My friend only wanted to pretend to have a lot of money. An argument erupted between the dealers and my friend. They jumped my friend, beating him nearly to death. They stole the money and left him to die in the alley. I was close enough to see everything and far enough away to not be noticed in the shadows. I sat there thinking it could've been me. It should've been me.

I still can't believe I chose that way of life instead of the way I was raised. My friend was in the hospital for over a week, and at one point he was not expected to live. My friends made excuses that it was everyone's fault but their own. It was easy for me to abandon responsibility for my own actions as well. The rule was: There are no rules. You just did whatever you wanted to do. "If it feels good, do it!" was the motto of the pack. *Pack* was a good word to describe that group of spoiled brats. As a group, they were unstoppable in their self-serving pursuit of pleasures. Alone, they acted almost civil.

Mr. Jones commands Mr. Smith to watch me, and then he and Mr. Brown step around the corner into the den. They seem to want privacy while discussing my future. Mr. Smith drags me along the same common wall as the den. He throws me against the return-air grate, scraping my face. "Bruce Willis, huh? Well, now you look a little more like the bloody character you're named after. But, Scout, you fight like a girl." Mr. Smith roars with laughter as blood drips from my cheek and ear.

Mr. Smith takes a chair at the table and sits down astraddle it. He crosses his arms over the back. He stares at me. I try to act limp and defeated so I can hopefully catch them off guard. My only hope will be surprise. I know I'm out numbered, and Mr. Smith is stronger than me, but I've seen smaller guys fight off greater odds when their lives are at stake.

I realize I can hear the men talking in the next room through the return-air vents in the wall. I sit very still, listening, with my head in my hands. They are going to town to get my dad, and then they are going to torture me to make my dad give them—

"Where's the remote for the TV, Scout?" Mr. Smith demands. I tell him it's on the kitchen counter, and I bury my head in my hands. Listening

18

again, I miss what it is they want, but that doesn't matter, because the next thing they say makes my blood run cold.

"That's what we'll do then. As soon as we get it, we'll get rid of them both. We'll pump the kid full of drugs, and it'll look like he killed his dad while he was tripping." The men return to the kitchen.

I look up and try to memorize their faces, their voices, their walk— anything that will help me to recognize them again. Why do my similar past brushes with the devil keep popping into my mind? A wave of guilt floods over me as I rack my brain, trying to remember if I have seen any of these men before. Maybe the familiarity is the devil himself.

It's hard for me to believe how stupid I was my senior year of high school and the two years in college before I flunked out. If it turns out that I have brought these demons to my family's doorstep, I will never be able to live with myself.

Mr. Jones is obviously the boss. He berates and talks down to Mr. Smith, and Mr. Brown does whatever he says. "Watch the Scout," he says to Mr. Smith. "Don't let him out of your sight. Don't let him move. Don't let him talk, Mr. *Super* Smith. We're going after the dad. Do you think you can manage this? You are the man for this job. It's *so* important, and that Scout is *so* dangerous, only a muscle-bound brain like you could be trusted with this job."

Mr. Jones and Mr. Brown exit the house, laughing. They continue to make fun of Mr. Smith as they get into the black Denali. I make a mental note that it has tinted windows. I can't see the tag from the floor where I sit, helpless. Mr. Smith jumps up to see the men out of the house. He only goes as far as the door so he can still reach me if he needs to do so.

"Thanks, guys. I won't let you down," Mr. Smith calls after them, smiling with pride.

I can't help but feel sorry for Mr. Smith. My sympathy doesn't last long, though. Mr. Smith walks over and kicks me hard and tells me to not cause him any trouble. I flinch and think about all the bruises I will have by morning. But what am I thinking? Bruises are the least of my worries. I have to get free, or my dad and I will be dead by morning.

19

Not That Bruce Willis!

Mr. Smith begins looking through the drawers in the kitchen and comes back with some duct tape. He tapes my wrists behind my back and puts some around my bare ankles. He chuckles a little as he flicks the palm trees' leaves on the flip-flops. "You don't look too dangerous, but I'm making sure you don't run off while I relax a little. I'm thirsty. What have you got to drink, Scout?" He saunters over to the kitchen and gets a glass and begins to look for something to drink.

"There's pop and juice in the fridge," I offer lamely.

Mr. Smith frowns and keeps looking. Maybe he wants liquor.

"Mr. Smith, there's a liquor cabinet in the next room," I say, thinking to myself that I can't be so lucky as to get Mr. Smith drunk. But I'll have a better chance of escaping if I can.

Mr. Smith looks interested. He comes back from the other room with a bottle. He begins to drink like a man who is dying of thirst. He drinks his liquor straight, over ice. It isn't long before he is on his third glass and is beginning to slur his speech.

I begin to plan. My stomach is already churning from the beans I ate this afternoon. When I get anxious, my stomach dumps lots of acid, and it gives me some kind of bad gas. My mom used to tease me about it. She said that if we could market that gas, we would win against any biological warfare.

Mr. Smith is beginning to warm up to me. I keep finding things to praise him about, because I see how he reacts when he has praise. Even when the other men gave him false compliments, Mr. Smith never recognized the sarcasm. I begin to belch loudly. I rock back and forth.

"I've got to go to the bathroom," I moan.

"No. Sit still and shut up," Mr. Smith says.

"Oh, please, I think I'm sick. I get nervous, and I get diarrhea really bad." This time I pass some gas.

"Kid, that's gross! Cut it out," he says as he pours another glass of straight liquor over ice.

"Please! Please! I'm going to make an awful mess in a minute. I don't think anybody will want to be in the house when I get sick." More gas escapes along with my mournful moaning. I watch Mr. Smith's response carefully.

"Oh, my gosh! You're not kidding! That's horrible!" Mr. Smith stands, pulls out a knife, and hesitates. I wonder if he is considering killing me or letting me go to the bathroom.

As if on cue, gas erupts from both ends. "It's an emergency now!"

Yanking me to my feet he spins me around and nicks my arm as he cuts the tape around my hands.

"Come on, and be quick. I want you back out here when they get back." Mr. Smith complains as he pulls me to the bathroom. I hop toward the bathroom that is adjacent to the outside. I moan and pass a little gas with each hop. Just as we get to the door I let another one rip. Mr. Smith nearly barfs. He shoves me in and shuts the door.

I moan and let the toilet ring hit the bowl. I grab my grandfather's knife from my pocket and cut my legs free. I grab my prescription antacid and take two pills. Then I look around for something to drop into the water of the toilet bowl. I find a jar of thick skin cream, and I grunt as I plop the cream into the toilet. Grabbing my stinky, manure-coated clothes from the hamper, I press them along the bottom of the door. I hear Mr. Smith stepping away, complaining about the rank odor.

"You need to see a doctor. That's disgusting!" Mr. Smith shouts as he puts distance between himself and the bathroom door. I hear him go to the liquor cabinet again for another bottle.

"Bruce Willis is also a man of cunning," I whisper to myself.

Chapter 3 - The Escape

I can't find any weapons in the bathroom. My only chance is to escape and go for help. I moan once more and empty the cream into the toilet. I open the cabinet that held my Scout shirt earlier and squirm through to the outdoor shower, almost losing my flip-flops in the getaway.

I sprint across the yard, keeping close to the edges where there are trees and scrubs. There is no way I can make it to the barn without being seen. I seem to be making an awful lot of noise running in my flip-flops, but I can't run on the dry sticks and grass without cutting the bottoms of my feet to shreds. Then the heavens begin to rumble louder than my flipping or flopping. It covers my rustling rush through the dry weeds and the cracking of dry sticks underfoot. The wind adds its own noise to the night. It is very dark now, perhaps eight or nine o'clock, with thick, dark clouds overhead. I'm breathing heavily, but the weariness I felt earlier in the evening has miraculously left me.

"Thanks, Lord!" I say as I glance to the sky.

Not That Bruce Willis!

I have to get to the ridge of the gorge at the back of the yard area. I begin running in the dense twilight. Far away, lightning lights the night dimly, giving me just enough light to be sure of my path. I know this yard like the back of my hand. I close my eyes and try to imagine what is coming up next in my path. The impending storm is upon me, and a gentle rain begins.

Mr. Smith calls out from the house, "Hey, Bruce, come back and I won't hurt you."

I sprint for my freedom as the thunder rumbles and lightning flashes. If I don't make it to the gorge before Mr. Smith looks out across this part of the pasture, I will stand out like a sore thumb on the barren landscape. I pick up the pace, plastic palm trees slapping at the top of my feet. The rain is coming down faster now.

Then my dad's face comes to my mind. I have to save both of us. With a heavy heart at the mere thought of losing Dad, I pick those flip-flops up and a put them down even faster. I'm high-stepping over the lower sagebrush and hurdling the smallest cedars, barely touching the ground. The image of that little desert lizard that can run across the hot sand on its hind legs comes into my mind. My back arches, and I step high, imagining my own legs churning. I wonder if that is what I look like, a hydroplaning lizard.

"Lord, please don't let my ADD get the best of me now. Help me to stay focused and find help up on the road. Please keep Dad safe. I don't deserve your protection, but I beg you to take care of him."

Thunder crashes and lightning electrifies the night with light, but it is too late. I am so preoccupied with thoughts of lizards that I don't see the edge of the ravine in time. I try to stop, but the heavens have opened up, and the chalky caliche has become a slime-like mud in which no one can remain upright. I peek over my shoulder and see Mr. Smith clearing the trees and looking across the pasture.

Gravity takes hold. Sliding at a breakneck speed, I'm skiing on my palm-tree-adorned flip-flops. I slide past the ravine's edge and sail like a cat falling out of a tree. My objective is to try and stay upright. I sail through the trees feet-first, losing my shoes and tearing holes in my sweats. Then I come to rest in the thick brush. It is brittle and pokes and scratches the rest of my body, but I'm in one piece with no broken bones.

Did Mr. Smith see me? I can't be sure, so I run again—this time without shoes, since they are somewhere in the trees. I stay on the cows' path because it will lead up out of the canyon to the windmill on top of the other side of the canyon, and the windmill is beside the road. I begin sprinting with each flash of lightning, but with the lightning comes rain. It washes the dried blood from my face, but it also makes the fresh wounds want to bleed again. I stop at the base of the cliff opposite the one I have just sailed from. I catch my breath and watch the top of the ridge for Mr. Smith. I want to stay in the security of the trees and scrubs, but I have to press on. My dad's life depends upon it. I don't see anyone, but I do hear something: a kind of gurgling, whooshing roar that I know I've heard before, but what is it? Suddenly I remember. It is a flash flood! The bottom of the canyon will soon be a death trap if I don't get up the side of this canyon to safety.

Looking up to the edge of the opposite cliff, I don't see anyone. I bow my head for a moment and thank God for pitching me off of the cliff. I am truly grateful. *I know you are with me and hear my prayers*, I pray. *Help me, Lord, to not be double-minded, believing in you one minute and doubting your power the next. I claim James 4:7–8 as one of your promises, Lord. "Submit yourselves, then, to God. Resist the devil, and he will flee from you. Come near to God and he will come near to you. Wash your hands, you sinners, and purify your hearts, you double-minded."*

I find the nearest cow path heading for the top of the canyon wall. I know God has been with me all along. If I'd had boots on instead of flip-flops, I still would have wiped out, but I also would've stopped sliding. Then Mr. Smith would have seen where I went and would be after me. I also know that the rain will wash out my tracks.

God is protecting me. Without my past experiences, I might've reacted differently to this situation. I know that God didn't want me to abandon my parents' training, but He can make everything work for His Glory. I haven't thought this much about God in years.

Not That Bruce Willis!

My mother's death shook me and everything I believed. I know now that I began to doubt God just so I could feel better about the things I was doing. I wasn't around when my mom was getting treatment my senior year. I was too busy sneaking out of the house and going to town to meet Cindy and her friends. But where was Cindy when my mom died? Where was she when I decided to sober up? Where was she when my funds dried up?

Cindy was my friend when I was a freshman in college, buying whatever her heart desired. She was a huge reason I chose to do what I did, but I take responsibility for my own actions now. My desires were my own.

I am buried in my thoughts, but I finally resurface to the here and now.

The ravines are filling with water and debris. I'm almost to the top. The lightning flashes more often, as if to light my path. I hear the flood just behind me now. It will erupt out of the canyon through the trees and brush any second. I don't have time to look back. I hold fast to my faith that I'll make it in time. I begin clawing my way to the top. The caliche is so slick now that I don't make any headway. The water is rising.

Has the Lord saved me from overdoses and fights just to take me now? Did He just want to give me the time I needed to return to Him? I don't know, but I'm not giving up. I believe God has me here for a purpose, and I must be ready to hear His voice.

I change how I'm climbing the canyon wall. To stay on the smooth mud paths is hopeless. I begin to brace myself on the roots and rocks. Slowly I rise out of the bottom, but the water rapidly gains on me. It is almost to my feet. One misstep and I'll drown. The lightning flashes, the roots of the small trees hold, and I'm up on top. I'm lying flat, catching my breath, when I hear a pickup truck. I gather strength that is no longer mine but that of a loving Father. As a verse from childhood enters my mind, I gather speed, running to intercept the pickup before it goes around the corner where I'll never catch it.

"I can do all things through Christ who strengthens me" (Phil. 4:13).

Interlude

Hemphill County Sheriff's Office

Ann and Rob arrive amidst chaos in the Hemphill County Sheriff's Office in Canadian, Texas. They smile at the sight. They step inside the sheriff's department and stand quietly to watch for a while. They remain slightly out of view of the dispatcher.

Ann has just come from the Performance Theater where a fire has broken out and caused everyone to be evacuated. A lightning strike is suspected. Ann places a lighter she no longer needs on the shelf.

Rob has just come from driving a truck on Highway 60. The road is blocked by an overturned truck carrying hazardous materials. The driver is nowhere to be found, and a vapor is leaking into the air. Highways 60 and 83 have been closed until hazard crews can get in place. Rob steps into the restroom to clean the mud from his boots.

The police band radio crackles to life.

Sheriff Taylor: "Sheila, what's the update? Did you call in all of the reserve officers? Have the neighboring counties responded yet?"

Dispatcher Sheila Carson: "Sheriff Taylor, there's been a fire at the Performance Theater. They're still accounting for the people inside. The fire departments from surrounding communities are responding to the fire as well. Preliminary findings believe it to be the lightning, but they can't be sure until daylight. The medical teams, including several hospitals, are preparing to receive multiple emergencies.

There is also a very strange wreck blocking highway 60 that has affected both highway 60 and 83. A truck has overturned and has hazardous

27

material on board. The first deputy to respond says that the driver is nowhere to be found. It's taking a long time to get the people in place who are trained to take care of such emergencies. Motorists are stranded and have been instructed to not get out of their cars because of possible contamination. There have been a few panicked motorists who thought they could drive down the medians and ditches. They're stuck in the mud.

Highways 83 and 60 are completely shut down just south of Canadian. The only ways into our town are from the east or north. We have requested more assistance at the Theater and the hazardous spill from the truck wreck sites, but the limited access will make it very time consuming for anyone to get to Canadian in a timely manner. The additional help from Wheeler and Miami to the south has to find alternative routes into Canadian. The streets are already beginning to fill with stranded motorists. The highways have been blocked since about six thirty. The relief dispatcher for our department lives in Miami. I know her town is in a neighboring county but she can't make it in to work. She says the highway is blocked, and the dirt roads are too slick. I've been on duty since six this morning, but I will stay as long as you need me. Do you know of anyone else who could help me?"

Sheriff Taylor: "No, sorry, Sheila. We will all have to pull extra hours tonight. I was on my way back to the office, but I will go to the site of the truck wreck. I may be needed on crowd control."

The day has been typical, but the late afternoon and evening have become a nightmare. There have been calls of possible break-ins, domestic disturbances, drunks on the street, kids toilet-papering a neighborhood. The whole county seems to have gone mad in this electrical storm. Sheila is overwhelmed because she is the only one left in the main office at Canadian. Everyone is needed elsewhere. She can't even get away long enough to go to the bathroom. The phones ring non-stop.

Ann wearing an identical dispatcher's uniform goes over to Sheila and asks if she can give her a break after she hangs up from talking to the Sheriff. Sheila is so relieved, she gladly leaves, asking when she should be back. Ann says she will cover the rest of the evening.

Rob remains in the bathroom until the dispatcher leaves. He steps out in a deputy's uniform. He had been wearing street clothes. He will be ready to go when and if a certain call comes through. Ann scans the call logs of yet-to-be-processed reports. She doesn't see what she is looking for and begins answering the phones. She keeps the available personnel running from one emergency to another. Rob and Ann hold the community's lives in their hands. They get a cup of coffee and settle in for the night.

Chapter 4 - Hope

The pickup fishtails and comes to a stop just before it runs over me. I know I must look like a crazy, bloody guy standing in the road. I am waving my monkey-long arms, jumping up and down, barefoot in the middle of the road. I rush up to the window and the men inside just look at me and discuss among themselves in Spanish whether or not to roll the window down. I yell through the window, "*Ayuda me*! Help me! I'm Bruce Willis!"

Oh, how I wish I'd paid more attention in Spanish class. *Ayuda me* is one of the only phrases I remember. I could ask them where the bathroom is, but that wouldn't help me much.

The conversation in the truck becomes quite animated. They all talk at the same time. It looks like they all want the driver to keep going. I understand a few words; *loco, cine, sangre.* I think maybe they are saying something about crazy, bloody actors or movies.

The driver rolls down the window a little and says, "I speak English. What do you want?"

"I'm Bruce Willis. I live over there. I need to call for help. Someone is trying to kill me. Please help me. Do you have a phone?" I shout over the storm and cursed my parents' addiction to action movies for the second time tonight.

The driver rolls up the window and speaks with the group. There are three guys in the backseat and one up front with the driver. He seems to be pleading my case to the others. The general consensus is to leave the *loco hombre.* I think they are calling me crazy again. The driver rolls down his window and hands me a cell phone. He tells me to make one call. I call 911. It seems like it takes forever to get an answer. A woman takes down my emergency. She says that lightning has struck the

Performance Center and there is a multi-car pile-up just outside of town. She asks, "Could I please get you to spell your first and last name? I don't think I heard you right."

I spell it out for her. "B-r-u-c-e W-i-l-l-i-s. I live out on South River Road. Some men came to our home and tied me up. I got away. My father is Mark Willis. You need to check on him too. He's at the Willis Cattle Company office outside of town. Some men mean to harm him. They intend to kill us! Please send help right away. It's urgent!"

She says, "We don't have time for prank calls. I'll send someone as soon as they're free. It will probably be morning, young man, and if this is found to be a prank, you will be punished to the full extent of the law." She pauses and then hangs up as I hear phones ringing in the background.

I can't believe what I hear. I told her it was a matter of life and death. I told her to go to the office and check on Dad. If she delays at all, we could both be dead by morning. I'm shaken from my numbness when the truck's horn scares me out of my wits. The driver demands his phone back. He rolls his window all the way down and snatches it out of my hand. I start to follow the phone into the cab of the truck, but the window is already closing. I barely get my hand back before it closes completely. I have to call a neighbor, someone close to help me. I step up on the running board and beg them to wait and help me. I say I have to get to the house in case my dad has returned. I have to save my dad, because the sheriff won't be out for a long time, if at all.

At the mention of the sheriff, the driver puts the truck in gear at the urging of his friends. I'm riding on the running board, pounding on the window, begging them to stay. They drive away, shaking their heads, calling out, *"Lo siento! No policia. No cine."* I jump away from the moving truck, slipping in the mud, thinking they said, "Sorry police movie." Did they think I was in a movie? Maybe they said, "No movie, no police." I don't know and I don't care. I have to get back to the ranch. It isn't long before the truck is out of sight.

As I sit at the edge of the road, I think to myself that I can't do this. Defeated, I think of Mom. She was so brave. She battled her cancer and never let it get her down. It was a hopeless situation for her, but she fought. She fought, not because she was afraid to die, but because she knew her family needed her. I begin to sob. The rain is pouring now and washes my salty tears into my cuts, making them sting. What can I do? And the answer comes to me:

"Jesus looked at them and said, 'With man this is impossible, but with God all things are possible" (Matt. 19:26).

I can't do anything, but with God all things are possible. I need to remember that I will not make the difference tonight. God will. Maybe those men haven't found my dad, and maybe they won't. But who am I kidding? I know my dad is at the office.

I begin walking down the road toward the ranch. I know the men will end up there sooner or later. I know they will find my dad.

I wasn't around to support my parents during their darkest moments. I wonder if this is the way Dad felt when he was trying to help Mom and me. I can't believe I could've been so selfish as to put him through such an ordeal. I'm going to be there this time and do everything in my power to support or save him. My actions have caused misery in the past, but no more. My previous choices were selfish. I thought the only one I was hurting was me. I was wrong. I never realized how much my actions affected those around me.

I was wasted when I returned to my apartment at college the night Mom died. I could hear the phone ringing as I unlocked the door. I answered and it was Dad. He was sobbing, telling me *he* was sorry. He had tried for hours to find me, but it was too late; my mother was gone. She had died two hours earlier. She wanted to say good-bye. She wanted to tell me herself that she loved me. Then she slipped away with my dad holding her and I wasn't even there.

I turn my face to the angry clouds, matching their passion. "I'm sorry, Mom! I'm so sorry! I love you, and I won't ever let you down again! God, please tell her. Please protect my dad. Show me what to do and where to go. I will follow You this time. I promise." I am screaming at the top of my lungs. It will not be my last prayer of the night.

Interlude

Hemphill County Sheriff's Office

Ann answers the phone, and a very excited young man on the other end begins to tell a tale of kidnapping, abduction, and possible murder. He wants someone to go to the Willis Cattle Company offices and get his dad. He wants someone to come to his ranch at once. She tries to explain to him that they are covered up with emergencies. She will relay the message, though. He gives her his name: Bruce Willis. She has him spell his name.

She turns, smiles, and nods for Rob to leave. He quietly leaves the building and gets into a truck with Hemphill County Sheriff's Department emblems and lights. Ann tells the caller that she knows he is pulling a prank. She will send someone later. Ann is all alone, and she will make sure it stays that way. The work load of emergency calls in front of her will see to that.

Ann opens a novel and begins to read as the night settles down around the room.

Chapter 5 - Ready? Action!

Okay, my choice is clear. I have to delay the strangers until the sheriff can arrive, and it sounds like it could be a long time. I feel the mud protecting my cut and bruised feet. It seems to make it easier to walk, so I try jogging. I notice that the rain has let up from the stinging torrents. It is a gentle, warm misting now. It seems to soothe the many cuts across my legs, arms, and face. *Thanks again, Lord,* I said with my heart as much as with my brain.

A car is making its way up the road from town. Help might be on its way. Then the clouds of doubt appear with the lightning overhead. What if the car is the Denali? I need to hide. I look around and find an outcropping of scrub cedar trees just a short distance from the road.

What if it's the sheriff? I decide I will be able to jump out in plenty of time to stop the car. Still, I'm certain it couldn't possibly be the sheriff after what the dispatcher has said. The sheriff couldn't get here this quickly from either disaster in town.

What if it's a stranger? Or it might be a neighbor. Should I try to flag down another passerby? They might be in danger as well if they help me.

The car is closer, and I crouch behind the trees. The headlights look like the GMC lights of the sheriff's department vehicles. I almost stand up. Sudden lightning flashes reveal that it is a GMC, but it is a black Denali. I hold my breath as it goes by and around the hill. I can hear the motor; it is still moving. I begin to jog toward the ranch again. I will have to be careful not to be seen. My pace slows, and I pause to get down on my knees.

Not That Bruce Willis!

"Dearest Lord, please help me to make it back to the ranch," I pray with my face turned up to the mist. "Please give me the wisdom to know what to do, to know what is *your* will and not mine. Please have the sheriff hurry. Thank you for the many times you have given me just what I needed."

As I approach the house, I think about disabling the cars so we'll all be here when the sheriff arrives. I can't let these intruders leave or get away. There's only the old farm truck and the black Denali. But if I disable them, I won't be able to get to town either. Suddenly I hear a whinny and a snort from behind the barn. I smile. The horses! We can use the horses!

My first plan is to disable the vehicles. I slip into the barn and grab a handful of sugar cubes to put in my pocket. I slip out of the barn and over to the Denali. The way it is parked, I can approach the side with the gas cap without being noticed from the house. I put sugar cubes into the gas tank of the Denali. Next, I return to the barn and take the coil from the truck. At least I hope it is the coil. In the movies, they always take off a little thingy with wires, and the car won't start. I hide it in the drawer of the workbench. I can always put the coil back on if my dad and I need a ride. Thunder rumbles low as if it's growling at the night.

I'm in the barn looking for something, anything that can be used as a weapon. Then I hear a shot and time stands still. My heart drops to the ground. Bile is rising in my mouth. I'm going to be sick. As my worst fears come into my mind, I vomit. Then I sprint and stumble across the property to the side of the house. I creep along the side of the house, getting closer to the window of the den. I look in a window and see Mr. Smith lying on the floor and my dad sitting in a straight-backed chair. My breath catches, and I slump to the ground sucking in air. I have been holding my breath without noticing.

Tears come into my eyes again, mainly from relief that my dad is alive, and then from guilt because I feel responsible for the life lost. I'm sure they killed Mr. Smith because I'm gone. I slowly stand up to peek in the window again. Mr. Jones and Mr. Brown are taping my dad's hands behind him. I have to think quickly. What can I use to protect my dad and myself? These men mean what they said earlier. They are going to kill Dad and blame me. They are probably going to make it look like I killed Mr. Smith too. If they killed one of their associates, they wouldn't hesitate to kill Dad.

I have been passive long enough; I have to man up and take action. I have a rifle and a pistol in my bedroom closet. They are for hunting, but my dad has also told me that if my family or I am ever threatened, to shoot now and ask questions later. I risk one more look to count heads. I see Mr. Brown over by the fireplace, working on the safe hidden behind a picture. Mr. Jones is waving a gun in my dad's face and slapping him after every sentence.

I creep to the back of the house. I climb the big cottonwood tree that grows outside my bedroom window. I can climb the tree as sure-footed as a cat, because I have gone out that way so many times in the past. Silently crossing the roof to the second floor window, I gently raise it. I listen at my closed bedroom door. There isn't a sound, so I go to my closet in the dark. I feel next to the door jamb and find my flashlight. It is small but gives off plenty of light. The blue halogen light shines across the pearly sparkles of the beadwork on my gun strap.

Not That Bruce Willis!

I sling the rifle across my back, and the hand-beaded strap my mother made crosses my heart. I take a moment to touch the beadwork and imagine her arms around me. I send a silent prayer to the Lord that what I am about to do is God's will and not my own. I grab matches, bullets, and my pistol, shoving them into my backpack. I wear the pack in front and start to climb out the window when I notice I've left wet footprints across the floor leading straight to the closet.

A slow creak brings me up short. That's the loose board on the stairs. Someone is coming! I have to leave. Hopefully, they won't see the tracks. I get out of the window as quietly as possible, but there is still noise. It will take a miracle for no one to hear me. As if on cue, thunder rumbles and doesn't let up until I'm in the tree making my way down. It masks any sounds I might've made. I keep to the shadows by staying close to the side of the house. I pass the breaker box, which gives me an idea. I run to the pole out by the barn, where the main electric feed to the whole ranch is. I pull the lever down, breaking the connection just as the heavens erupt in a light display. The whole ranch is thrown into darkness. The loss of electricity will appear to be a product of the storm's rage. "Thank you, Lord, for showing me what to do and when to do it," I say in a whisper to my constant companion.

I move through the night to the backyard. I choose the low-hanging branches of the apple tree, where the girth of the trunk is more than wide enough to hide behind. I rest my rifle on one of the lower branches and aim it at my bedroom window. I watch through my night scope, which enhances even the smallest light present to illuminate everything. I never hunt at night, but I like to watch for my prey at dawn and dusk when there is little light.

There is a pinpoint of light in my room. Someone has entered it, and they are looking around. The light sweeps the floor, and moves to the far side of the room. They are in the closet. The light comes back into the room and sweeps across the floor leading to the window. The window! I've left the window open! They will know someone has been there because of the wet footprints and the window being open. A shadow of a man stands in the window, looking out. With no light to give away any of the features of the yard, he can't possibly see me. His gaze lingers on the apple tree. He can only guess where I might be. What will he do to my dad, now that they know I'm here? Will they use my dad to lure me out? Should I go?

A crack of thunder scares me, it's so close. It seems to say a resounding *no!* I stand perfectly still and watch the window, with my rifle sighted in on the shadow. The man leans down. Lightning begins to flash, dimly at first, then building. It begins to brighten the night. The man scans the landscape in the lightning flashes. He watches, moving his field of vision slowly across the rain-soaked ground. He sees the footprints in the mud. He leans forward, then out of the window for a better look. His gaze is following the footprints as they lead right up to the apple tree. He draws his gun, gripping it in both hands, aiming.

The lightning flashes, and my eyes begin to sight down the barrel of the gun as he concentrates on the tree. I have him in my cross-hairs. My finger is on the trigger, pulling it snugger all the time. Then the heavens unload all of their fury upon the earth. The lightning is blinding and the thunder deafening. A shot sounds, and pieces of splintered tree bark sting my face, causing me to flinch. I pull the trigger a split second later, and the rifle fires. Both shots ring out nearly in unison with the bellowing thunder.

I look away and then back through the scope and see Mr. Brown slumped out of the window. He is lying half in and half out. There is a dark rivulet winding its way down the white shingles. It mixes with the torrents of rain and turns lighter until it's so diluted I can no longer see it. By the time it drips from the roof top, it is washed clean. I grab the tree trunk to keep myself from collapsing, and I see where Mr. Brown's bullet has hit the tree. It is right next to my head. I sit down hard and suck in some air as the world spins out of focus for a moment.

"Brown! Brown, where are you?" I can hear Mr. Jones calling from the den. "Get down here and stop your prowling around! We got business to finish."

I pull myself upright. The unfinished business is the killing of my father.

I grab my rifle and take off around the house to the front yard. I set up at the corral fence behind the feed bunkers. I aim my rifle toward the den window and find my dad. He is bleeding, still taped to the chair.

Not That Bruce Willis!

Mr. Jones draws a knife and circles Dad. I rest my rifle on the fence to keep it steady, and I put a bullet in the chamber. I am scared to death that I might hit Dad, since they are so close together. Mr. Jones cuts the tape from my dad's hands. They walk over to the fireplace. They are out of sight. I can't see them! What is happening?

I move, but in doing so, I have made myself visible to Mr. Jones if he looks out the window. The men are at the safe. My dad is opening it. The safe is open. Mr. Jones won't need Dad anymore. He pockets the cash. There isn't much cash kept at the ranch since I was so irresponsible in the past. I stole from anyone, whenever and wherever I got a chance.

Mr. Jones gets some papers out of the safe. I'm sure they are just wills, deeds, and the like, because my parents didn't keep anything like bonds at the house either. I am slowly walking closer and closer to the house. If I'm going to be out in the open, I'm going to be close enough not to miss. As close as Mr. Jones and my dad are standing together, I'm still afraid to shoot.

I move around, separating the two men in my scope. Mr. Jones puts the papers into a briefcase. He turns and walks right up to Dad and begins shouting in his face. Dad looks shocked by whatever is said. Mr. Jones backhands him across his face, spinning him around and knocking him down. The coast is clear. I have the shot I need. I'm lined up with Mr. Jones's right side, but I hesitate. Mr. Jones raises his right hand with the gun. He aims the gun at the floor, and I can only assume it's at my unconscious dad. I take a breath, hold it, and fire. Mr. Jones falls forward.

I run into the house, sprinting cautiously from room to room, until I'm sure Mr. Jones isn't moving. Sure enough, the bullet has found its target, and Mr. Jones is shot through the rib cage and his heart. Crawling out from under the fallen corpse is my dad.

I drop my rifle onto the couch and gather my dad into my arms. We cry, holding each other, saying nothing at first. Then Dad says that there is still a man upstairs, that we have to hide. I tell him the other man won't be bothering us.

We check to make sure each man is dead. They are. We don't want to stay in the house. We try the phones and find they are disconnected. The men probably cut the lines earlier in the evening. We go out to the bunkhouse. Years ago, it was used by the hired hands who helped with the ranch. Now it is used for guests during hunting season. There are a shower, clothes, cookstove, medicine cabinet, and bunk beds. It's almost dawn. I realize how exhausted I am and head out the back door. I grab a cell phone off the bar as I go by.

"I think we should call the sheriff again, Dad," I say, handing him the phone, "only this time I want you to call. I don't have much luck getting anyone to take me seriously. As soon as I tell them my name, they stop listening and think I'm joking. I'll explain later."

Interlude

Hemphill County Sheriff's Office

Ann answers the phone: "Yes, what is your emergency?"

Mark Willis says, "There has been a murder. Send the sheriff as soon as possible to the Willis Ranch. Some strangers broke into my home and threatened my son. They kidnapped me in town and brought me out here to kill me. They were going to rob us and kill us. We had to shoot them in self-defense."

Ann asks, "Did they get away with any valuables?"

Mark explodes, "Are you not listening? They tried to kill us! Forget the robbery. Get out here!"

Ann says in a monotone, "Your call has been logged, and we will send someone as soon as we can. I don't have to listen to that tone. Good-bye, sir."

Ann deftly deletes Mark's call from the call log just as she did earlier to the call from the Willis boy. She turns off the surveillance cameras, takes the tape out, and takes it with her. She looks around and wipes down everything that she and Rob have touched. Then, wiping the doorknobs clean, she leaves the phones ringing, locks the door, and closes it.

Chapter 6 - The Unbelievable

Dad just stands there, looking at my phone. "I can't believe the stupidity of some people. Out of everything I said, all she got was that there had been an attempted robbery. She was offended by my tone and hung up on me. You wait until we clean up. We're going to town, and I'll give that office a piece of my mind!"

"Now I don't feel so bad," I say. "I was so frustrated with her when I called. I know they were busy, but surely if a murder is being committed, they can take the call. I got the same answer; they said they would send someone as soon as they could, right?"

"Well, maybe we're a little wound up," Dad replies. "I'm taking a shower. Then I'll lie down until you're finished. And then we're heading to town, whether the roads are passable or not."

"Okay," I say. "I just want to lie down. Forget about a shower." I stretch out on one of the bottom bunks.

My mind is spinning as I think about how we will get to town. The roads will be nearly impassable after all the rain we've received. The caliche base on the roads is slick as snot. Thinking of all the scratches and scrapes I got sailing off the canyon rim in the mud, I figure the roads might as well be slime. Whatever direction gravity pulls you is the direction you'll take, whether you're headed that way or not. A gentle rain continues to come down, making a soothing, rhythmic tapping on the tin roof. Everything slows way down, and I fall sound asleep.

Mark comes out of the shower and looks at his sleeping son. He stands by the window and watches the rain clean away the grime from the window, thinking of the filth that has entered their lives tonight. He starts a pot of coffee and tries to make sense of the evening.

Not That Bruce Willis!

His employees left the feedstore early because it's Friday, there's a big football game, and most of them have kids in school. Mark was in his apartment watching the news when he heard someone in the office. He was sure he had locked all the doors. He poked his head out the apartment door to see who was there, and someone hit him on the back of the head.

When he came to, he was in the back seat of an SUV with darkened windows. When they stopped at the ranch, he was surprised. Why would someone kidnap you just to take you home? The night was a blur after the kidnappers shot the man who was at the house. The man had apparently let Bruce get away.

Mark looks at his sleeping son who is so precious to him. He smiles and can't wait to hear how Bruce managed to get away. After the murder of their partner, Mark took everything the two men said seriously. He prayed that Bruce was far away and safe. Personally, Mark didn't care whether he himself lived or died. Ever since Theresa passed away, he has been pretty much counting the days until he can be with her.

He has thought his son doesn't need him, but he now knows that he is mistaken. Bruce *does* need him. He will always need his dad, no matter how old he is, and from today forward Mark will start acting like a dad again. He has been given a second chance, and he isn't going to blow it.

I wake up, startled at first. Then I see my dad staring down at me. I realize I am in the bunkhouse and the night's events cover me again.

"It hurts even to smile," I say to him. "I think I'm going to take a shower after all and put some ointment on these cuts. Boy, that coffee smells good. Thanks, Dad." Seeing my dad's warm eyes smiling down on me fills me with emotion. "I haven't told you lately, Dad, but I love you, and I am so sorry for—"

Dad puts his hand over my mouth. "Don't say a word," he says. "I love you too. Just go clean up, and I'll help you doctor those cuts. I've got plenty to be sorry for too. Let's just start over." He gives me a gentle hand out of the bed and sends me toward the bathroom.

Mark has to step out of the fog he has been content to walk around in this past year. Things happen around him every day, but he hasn't noticed any of them.

What happened after the first man was shot? What was it they wanted out of the safe? Was that all they wanted? Did he know these men? They didn't seem all that interested in the money—only the papers.

What papers are in the safe? Nothing he can think of that would interest anyone. There are just his will, the deed to the land, and oil well papers—all things that are of no value except to the Willises. But the man with the gun looked like he'd hit the mother lode when he saw the papers. He put them in a briefcase and planned on taking them. The man didn't seem as stupid as to think that he could possibly do anything with them. What did the guy say just before hitting him? Something about a jackpot? Was that right?

None of it makes any sense.

I come out feeling much better without the dried blood all over me. By the time the coffee pot is empty, the sun is breaking through the clouds and the rain has ended. We try to get the truck to start, but in my zeal to disable it, I have loosened more than I intended. Things always work out in movies. Real life is rarely like that. Bruce Willis would have made it work in the movies. But, I have to face it, I'm not that Bruce Willis.

Chesterfield whinnies from the meadow. We look at each other and head toward the barn. I stop off at the bunkhouse long enough to pick up my backpack, where I have a few sugar cubes left for him. Dad and I saddle the horses, and we're on our way within fifteen minutes. If someone has been dispatched from the sheriff's office, then something has gone wrong. Either they have run off the road, or something or someone is blocking it. We head across the pasture. Most of the time, we stay near the road. We watch for signs of where a vehicle may have skidded off the road in the storm. Not more than a couple of miles from the house, we see the deputy's pickup in the ravine.

We dismount and run over to the truck. The driver's door is open, and the radio is popping to life. We listen as someone is asking for a report. A man identifying himself as Deputy Lowe replies that he has arrived at the Willis' ranch. No one is there, but there are three dead men. They have no identification. They appear to have been picked off with a rifle from outside the house. Someone is a pretty good shot. He has hit each man with one shot and killed him. He wasn't planning on missing. It was obviously premeditated.

Deputy Lowe continues to report that there aren't any vehicles except a truck. Money and drugs are scattered around one room in the home. It looks like a drug deal gone bad. There is no sign of the family. The deputy says he thinks the kid is probably strung out and paranoid and shot at anything in his sights, that the kid just sat outside and picked these men off one at a time.   He says that if the dad was there, he is probably dead too. He expects they'll find the dad's body in the canyons with a rifle bullet in him. The boy's room has been invaded. A man was trying to escape the house and was shot there.

"I can't believe what you're telling me," says the sheriff's voice over the radio. "Is there a gun in the boy's room?"

"No, sir. No gun," the deputy replies. "The safe in the den has been emptied as well."

"I'll be right out there," says the sheriff. "Don't leave the ranch, and don't touch anything."

Dad picks up the microphone and tries to respond to the sheriff, but the radio seems to be broken. We can hear the conversations, but we can't transmit. Neither one of us has thought to pick up the cell phone from the bunk house. We need to go back to the ranch and set the deputy straight on what really happened. We mount up and head back across the pasture toward the ranch.

As we ride, I ask Dad, "Did the men get out drugs when you were there? I swear to you, Dad, I was not messing with drugs. There weren't any drugs when I left the house. Mr. Smith was drinking heavily, but it was from your liquor cabinet. Dad, I swear, I haven't touched any drugs since Mom's funeral, and I didn't know these men."

"I believe you, Son. That's not what bothers me. There weren't any drugs, and I know you haven't been doing drugs. And the only money was the money that Mr. Jones put in his pocket. As far as I know, it's still in his pocket. It didn't fall out, I'm sure of it. There's another thing the deputy said. He said there weren't any guns. But two of the three men had guns. And what happened to the Denali? These men didn't just appear! Now it looks like they came to the house in our truck, and you and I know that's impossible. Do you know a Deputy Lowe?"

"No, I don't know a Deputy Lowe, but I have tried to stay clear of the law. I guess Mr. Brown's gun could have slid down the roof and into the shrubs. Mr. Jones's gun could be under the couch. I don't remember Mr. Smith having a gun, just arms as big as cannons. But I'm positive I left my rifle on the couch."

We ride in silence, deep in our own thoughts. Before either of us realizes it, we are at the ranch. We are at the back of the property, coming up the very ravine I sailed off of last night. Dad insists on going to the deputy alone. There seems to be a dark cloud of doubt across his face.

"This new deputy seems to have already made up his mind about what happened," Dad whispers. He may shoot you and ask questions later. I want you to hide here in the locust grove at this wash out. If things get out of hand, you can be out of sight and down the ravine at a moment's notice. I'm sure I can straighten this out. No matter what happens, promise me you will stay clear."

"I promise, Dad," I whisper back. "Please be careful."

I watch my dad ride into the yard and call out as he dismounts. "Hello, there! I'm Mark Willis, and this is my home. Are you the deputy sent to help us?"

"Yes, I'm the deputy *waiting* for you."

The man pulls my own rifle up to his shoulder and takes aim at Dad. I'm sure it's my rifle because of the beadwork strap.

"Stop!" Dad holds up his open palms, dropping the reins. "I'm not the intruder. I'm the owner. I've got identification." As the deputy starts to squeeze the trigger, Dad drops to the ground and lies flat behind the bunk feeders inside the corral.

Not That Bruce Willis!

The deputy's shot hits just past Dad's shoulder and spooks his horse. Dad ducks behind an outcropping of rocks as his horse rushes past, then crawls toward the ravine. I have already skidded to the bottom where I'm waiting for him. Dad hops on Chesterfield behind me, and we take off at a trot. We stay in the heaviest vegetation, even though at this time of year, there isn't much.

"Where do we go?" I ask, knowing we only have a few minutes before the deputy will come after us.

"I don't know, but I do know even a city boy could track this big old horse's tracks. We're sinking in pretty deep. Let's let him go as soon as we can get on some rock and make some time on foot. What do you think?" Dad asks.

"Sounds perfect," I say, "and I think I know where we can go. How about the cave up on Wolf Creek? You said that only our family knows about it. At least your horse is somewhere ahead of us, so the deputy can't use him to ride after us. Without a horse or vehicle, it will take him a while to catch up to us."

"This whole affair is a nightmare!" Dad says with concern. "It is just unbelievable. I would think I was dreaming, but we couldn't both be having the same nightmare."

We ride for at least two hours, meandering down the larger ravines. We always head northeasterly toward the cave, but by twisting and turning, it should appear that we are just running for our lives. We come to some hard ground that's in the middle of the pasture and far away from any roads. Dad dismounts first, and then I get off and unsaddle Chesterfield. It is well after noon. I take his halter off so he won't become tangled in anything on his way home, which is where he will eventually go.

There is no more talking as we sprint across the prairie, watching the road and lying flat when we see cars. It has taken most of the morning and afternoon, but we finally come to Wolf Creek. We pause and get a drink from the spring water that seeps from the porous rocks of the Ogallala Aquifer. The aquifer comes close to the surface in a few places, feeding Wolf Creek and keeping the water flowing year round. We follow the creek to a grove of locust trees in a bottom. The cave is just under the rim of cap rock, hidden by a group of cedars. Because of the creek, there is more vegetation and wildlife that lives here in this small valley. The face of this plateau faces west.

"What have you got in that backpack, Son?" Dad asks.

"I've got a flashlight, Grandpa's pocket knife, a pistol with no bullets, some bullets for my rifle, matches, and two sugar cubes for Chesterfield," I respond. "I just wish I had some food."

Interlude

Hemphill County Sheriff's Office

The sheriff leaves the office, and the department is trying to piece together just what has happened the night before. The fire with its mysterious origin and causalities, and the wreck with its hazardous materials and missing driver kept all agencies busy. They try to figure out who was where. Wasn't Sheila on duty yesterday?

Sheila comes around the corner after getting the coffee brewing. All eyes are on her when she sits down at her desk. "What?" she asks.

"Where are your logs from last night?" the office manager asks. "We need to know who went where and when they were called out."

"I didn't work last night," she answers. "I worked yesterday from 6 a.m. to 8 p.m. I didn't even have a break all day."

"Then who was on duty last night?"

"Ann, I think, is what the name tag on her shirt said."

"We don't even have an Ann on staff. Who are you talking about?"

"She came in and asked if I was ready to be relieved. She said she would take the night shift. Since I hadn't even had time to go to the bathroom, I said sure. She was dressed in a shirt like mine with her name on it. She seemed to know what she was doing. It was so hectic, I just thought that you had called in someone from another county."

"Check with all personnel and see if anyone knows this Ann," says the office manager. "Then check other counties that were helping last night. See if they sent someone. Check the cameras. Maybe we can get a picture of Ann, and someone will recognize her."

After a lengthy discussion among all the office workers, they agreed that no one had called in reinforcements. They began to call the neighboring county agencies to ask if they had sent an Ann over to help out.

"There isn't any tape in the cameras," the janitor says.

Chapter 7 - Visions

The cave is one of my favorite places on the ranch, not just because of the memories here but because of the history it represents. The cave is in solid rock with petroglyphs on the walls, drawn by early travelers. I look at the cave this time from the viewpoint of how much protection it will provide us. It is up under the cap rock, giving us a great vantage point. It is within walking distance from the spring, so we'll have fresh water. Normally we wouldn't want to stay here because of the rattlesnakes. Hopefully, the snakes are making their way to their dens for winter by now. The vegetation in front of the cave is comprised of scrub cedars and sagebrush. It completely hides the cave. Paths leading up to and away from the cave are at very gradual angles, instead of the usual deep vertical cuts that the erosion makes. There is a natural ledge that runs in front of the entrance in both directions.

Before leaving the security of the locust groves at the bottom, we scan the horizon to see if we're being followed. We wait about an hour and see no one. We begin our ascent to the cave. Since the cave faces west, the sun is riding low, and we should be able to see if any animals have moved in. The cave is the size of a small, two-man tent. It is about eight feet by eight feet with a roof of five feet at its highest point. Using my flashlight, I check the edges for napping rattlesnakes.

"Hey, Dad, look what I found, my old Fossil Watch box. Let's see what's in it."

Dad smiles and sits down cross-legged on the floor of the cave. I join him, but I'm stiff, and to sit cross-legged makes the scabs on my many cuts open again. I settle for lying down on my belly. We are a couple of feet inside the opening so my feet hit the wall. I open the box and take out a compass.

Not That Bruce Willis!

"I remember getting this when I was eight and I'd learned all of my memory verses for that year. We came up here, and you had a ceremony to present it to me. I think that was the first year we came to the cave together. It meant so much to me."

"Bruce, the memory work was meant to help you when life threw you a curve ball, so you would be able to catch it and know where to turn," Dad says affectionately. "You can always rely on God. He is always there. The compass represented the direction you should always go—the direction that God chooses for you."

"Dad, at eight years old, I didn't understand just how important it was, but now I do. I've started praying again. I know when Mom died I said I'd never pray again. But I think it was the drugs talking. I said that when I was blaming everyone and everything—except myself—for what happened in my life. I asked the Lord to help me last night, and He did. When I couldn't help making noises, He covered the sounds with thunder. He gave me lightning when I needed to see in the dark. God gave me the push I needed to pull the trigger. I know God led me. Now, where *He* leads, I will follow. But I really don't know what is going on now."

"I don't understand everything either," Dad says. "Let's take a break from thinking about what has happened and get our minds off it. We're exhausted and hungry, and we might have better luck if we think about it tomorrow when we're fresher. What else is in that box?"

I lay out three perfect, small arrowheads for shooting small game. I also have a slightly larger one with a broken edge and some rawhide twine wound around a stick. I reach into the bottom and pull out a small picture. I read the back. It says, *friends 4 ever.* I turn it over, and there is Cindy smiling back at me. The cave seems to spin for a minute. I close my eyes tight to hold back the memories of failed love and betrayal. I let my weary head droop a little.

"Dad, I really loved her, and I thought we'd be together forever like you and Mom. I can't believe that I reconnected with her after all those years to find that she had another love—drugs and alcohol. In this picture, Cindy is sweet, innocent, and a little daring. I liked that. But she became more daring as she grew older. When mom was diagnosed with cancer

54

and started her treatments, I saw how short life could be and decided to get Cindy to notice me. I've always been shy with girls. When I decided to live life on the edge, I went all the way. I didn't say *no* to anything. I just failed to realize at the time that the people pushing me to the edge didn't really care about me. They only wanted to see me crash. They didn't care about me; they just wanted my money." The vision of how I had been used became clear. "I would do almost anything just to be included."

I can't believe I'm saying all this aloud. I feel like I'm in a trance, recognizing for the first time the real people behind the kids I called friends. It's like a veil has been lifted, and I can see clearly their true motives.

"I'm sorry, Son. Is she a part of your life now?"

"No. Yes. Well, sort of. At the end of our high school years, we began to date. We stayed together through college. I told her I was going to clean up my act and get off the drugs. I begged her to join me. She left me for some rich, old dude."

I realize Cindy never wanted to be my girlfriend. It's embarrassing to admit it to myself, even without saying it aloud to my Dad. Most of the time she was so wasted she didn't even know I was there. Somehow I feel stronger just facing the truth. I can see the players for who they really are and not get tied in knots. The past four years become very clear.

"Were you close in college?" Dad asks.

"We were more than friends, Dad. I thought we would get married, but I couldn't see how messed up she really was. I was pretty strung-out too. I really cared for her, but she only cared about what I could buy her."

I feel a little better. I know this probably shocks my dad, but after all of my escapades in college, he probably isn't surprised. I keep my eyes and head down. The stone floor is beginning to hurt my hip bones. I sit up, move to the cave opening, and stand. I watch as the last sliver of sun slides behind the horizon.

"We'd better gather a little firewood while there's still a glow of light in the sky," I say, starting down the path.

Mark follows, thinking about how much his son has revealed to him. He knows that Bruce probably feels like he's taking a huge chance in telling him. As they pick up sticks in silence, Mark thinks about how he has been less than supportive or understanding when Bruce landed in trouble over and over again in college. He never knew his son felt so wounded, that he was dealing with everything alone. Mark will have to think about the right thing to say. No, he will *pray* for the right things to say.

Lord, you know the heart of my only child. Show me what to do and what to say. If you have given us this time together to save both of us, please help us to use it fully to your Glory. Amen.

Mark raises his bowed head and finds his arms full of firewood, so he heads back to the cave. He sets his sticks down and picks up the arrowheads. Then he heads back down the trail to find a straight stick and attaches an arrowhead to it. If he gets close enough, he might be able to wound a prairie chicken and catch it. He has seen where some were going to roost as he gathered sticks earlier.

He returns a couple of hours later. The night is dark, with only a half-moon lighting his way. He smells the smoke of Bruce's fire before he sees the flames. The two chickens he has managed to get are cleaned and rinsed off at the stream.

"I'm impressed, Dad," I say as he returns. "That looks wonderful, even raw. I thought I knew what you were up to when you took the arrowheads, but I wasn't sure. I'm surprised you got two."

"Well, to be honest," says Dad, "I only got one with the arrowhead. The other one had a broken wing and couldn't get away. I guess we were just in luck tonight."

"I think God provided the second bird," I say, smiling. "He knew we were hungry. I'm beginning to see His work in my life again."

"I believe you're right about His hand in all that we do," Dad says. God definitely provides what we need. Sometimes it's not what we want. Your mother was more than ready to go to heaven to live with her Lord and Savior. I wanted her to stay with me for selfish reasons, but I really wouldn't want her here in pain. God knew what she needed."

I see that Dad understands, maybe for the first time. I hope that one day I will have that kind of understanding of why God took my mom.

I silently wish Dad would say something about what I've just revealed to him about Cindy and my choice to walk away from everything that I was raised to believe. I really need his forgiveness.

"Son, I've been thinking about what you said earlier," Dad says, "and I want you to put that time in your life behind you. I said in the bunkhouse that we are starting over. The past is the past. I am so sorry you had to live that part of your life without the support of your parents. I am here now. I love you. I trust you. If you need to talk about this girl, I will listen. I promise not to say a word unless you want me to.

"I know we will get through all of this. You had nothing to do with what has happened to us. It was just some greedy men wanting whatever they could steal. I don't understand it, but we will make sense of it together. From now on we will do everything together. As far as your girlfriend, I'm sorry it didn't work out. I wish I knew why some people think we all have to behave as society dictates and not by what the Bible says. All I do know is that there is a constant war for our souls being waged every minute of every day. I know whose side I am on, because I know how the war ends."

I look up after his first sentence. I can't believe how lucky I am to be forgiven. My Dad has forgiven me. My Heavenly Father has forgiven me. I feel their love and am grateful.

"The fire is burned down to coals," I say with a lighter heart. "Let's make a rotisserie. I'll do the cooking, and you can have the dishes."

The smoke spirals out of the opening and up to the heavens. It's so fragile, and yet it can lift the burdens of souls. Both of us sleep peacefully all night.

Not That Bruce Willis!

Interlude

Hemphill County Sheriff's Office

Sheriff Taylor listens to the powerful strangers. They have credentials from the government. They look official, but they sound ridiculous as far as Sheriff Taylor is concerned. They are taking over the entire investigation of the Willis family. They give strict orders that no one is to pursue any leads. All information is to be turned over to them immediately.

"I don't understand why this is a matter of homeland security," says Sheriff Taylor. "It is ridiculous to think that the Willis family is involved in anything that will harm our government. They are the victims of a very violent crime, I'm sure of it!" His conviction is clear.

The sheriff hasn't been allowed to view the scene of the crime. The men in black suits had the driveway blocked off when he arrived that morning. They refused to let him past. He has been cut off from all resources that could possibly help him. They have sealed all documents, logs, phone files, and surveillance footage all over the entire town. Everyone in authority over him has told him to back off. They say there is strong evidence that drugs were involved. Sheriff Taylor can't believe that Bruce has backslid, but he guesses it's possible. He is not allowed to ask any questions.

He isn't going to hand over this investigation to outsiders if he can help it. He isn't sure what's happened, but he is sure that his friends are innocent. The sheriff and Mark were deacons at the same church, and their kids grew up together. It's true that Bruce went through a rough patch for a few years, but he is a different man now. Taylor would like to give him the benefit of the doubt. But these strangers seem to already have their minds made up and the outcome already planned.

Not That Bruce Willis!

"Sheriff, here are your orders," says a Mr. Johnson in a matter-of-fact way. "We are now the department in charge, and we are telling you and your men to back off and stay out of our way. If you have any information about either of the Willis men, we expect you to tell us immediately. We will be releasing a statement to the press this morning. We will be responsible for all press releases concerning this matter. If you should be approached by any reporter, you are to refer them to us. You are to make no comment. I repeat that you are not to be involved in any way—no behind-the-scenes questions, nothing! You are not to go to the ranch or to Willis' office. Understood?"

"I understand completely," Sheriff Taylor says and leaves the room. If he doesn't, he will surely give Mr. Johnson a tongue-lashing that will cost him his job. He won't be able to help Mark and Bruce if he's fired. He has to work quietly—and only with trusted Christian brothers who know how to keep their mouths shut and not gossip. Sheriff Taylor knows in his heart that Mark Willis would not stop looking for him if the circumstances were reversed. Something is wrong, and he is going to find out just what it is—or lose his job trying. He will visit some of the Willis' neighbors and let the Lord lead him to where he needs to go.

Chapter 8 - Friends or Enemies

The sun is well into the morning sky when Mark wakes up. Bruce is sleeping. Mark walks out of the cave so he can straighten up and stretch. The cave is a gift from God, but it's a little cramped for two six-foot-plus men. He thinks of the times he has come to this very cave with his own dad. They are his best memories of his dad. He and his dad made time once a year, every year, to come up to the cave and spend a week. The trips were usually in the fall about this time of year. They checked the water as they were getting ready to go into winter with the herd. If the water supply was plentiful, they would keep all of the calves. If it was marginal, they would sell off all of the larger calves and keep only the smallest. Even though it was mainly open range, there were still the outer boundary fences to check. There were also fences between the summer and winter pastures.

Mark and Bruce began their own father-and-son tradition at the cave when Bruce was eight. Mark feels the pang of guilt again as he thinks about having missed that opportunity with his son this fall. In fact, he has not come up here with Bruce for several years.

His own dad proudly told him time and again how he would inherit all of this land one day. Mark wonders why he has refrained from ever telling Bruce that he will one day own this entire ranch. Back when he was younger, he was always uncertain about how to respond to his dad's words. Maybe that's why he has never said those same words to his son. He knows now, as a man, what he would say to his father. He would tell his dad to share the wealth with his sister. Maybe that issue was the reason for his silence. But with his own son, there is a difference; Bruce has no siblings.

Not That Bruce Willis!

Bruce is an only child. Mark and Theresa tried but were never blessed with another child. They were so thankful for Bruce. The doctors told them it was a miracle that they had their son. Mark remembers when he and Bruce stopped coming to the cave together; it was Bruce's sophomore year. Theresa wasn't feeling well, and they were beginning their nightmare of finding out that she had cancer.

Mark walks up on the ridge and looks out over the land. He turns slowly, taking in the panoramic beauty. Mark's dad was a boy when *his* dad had told him of the Great Panhandle Oil and Gas Field. Beneath his feet, the various companies have taken out billions of dollars' worth of gas and oil over the years. This resource has made the companies and landowners rich beyond their wildest dreams. There is still gas and oil to be taken from the area. Mark is grateful for the life this resource has afforded him and his family, but sometimes the cost has been more than he wanted to pay. He knows this when he thinks of his son and how the excess almost killed him. God has blessed him, and he must be a trustworthy steward of this gift.

I crawl to the opening, pull back a limb, and look out across this beautiful land. I wonder where Dad has wandered off to, but I'm not worried. The birds seem to sing tranquility into the day. I smile, bow my head, and thank God for our safety, the beautiful land, the spring-fed water, and the rain-fresh, clean air. I'm still hungry, but I know beyond a shadow of a doubt that God will provide us with what we need. I feel so unworthy, but I know that *no one* is worthy. God accepts us by His Grace, not because anyone has earned it. All I have to do is go to God in prayer.

I begin to confess my sins. I not only stopped going to church when I went off to college, I also stopped praying. I have a lot of catching up to do. I see Dad's shadow move across the trees. He must be on the cap rock above me. My quiet sobs can be heard by both of my fathers—the one in Heaven and the one standing on the rock above the cave. The shadow of my Dad sits down. He bows his head. Somehow I know we are both praying for wisdom to know what to do, where to go, and whom to trust. I end my prayer and join Dad up top.

"Why didn't you wake me?" I inquire as my head pops over the edge of the cap rock. I pull myself up and look at the view my dad has been admiring.

"I thought you needed the sleep," Dad says. "Since you're awake, let's talk about what we should do next."

Then a noise catches our attention. It's a helicopter. It's far away, over by the ranch. It seems to be making ever widening circles with the ranch being the center.

"Dad, do you think they are looking for us?" I say, first hopeful and then fearful. "Should we flag them down? Or maybe we should hide."

"I think that until we know for sure who our friends and enemies are, we should get off this ridge," Dad says. "Let's go down into the cover of those trees until we figure out what to do. We need to make sure there isn't any smoke coming from last night's campfire." He sprints to the edge and jumps down to the natural ledge of the red shale.

After dousing the fire and retreating to the security of the cave, we discuss our next step. "I think we should sit still one more day," Dad says. "Something still bothers me, and I can't put my finger on it. I mean, besides the obvious. There's a deputy that neither of us knows. The Denali, the guns, and probably the IDs of those men are gone. Anything and everything that might tell us who they were or who is behind this—it's all missing."

"I'm with you," I say. "I can't explain it, but something tells me when to stay away from people. No, that's not true; it's more like I have this strong need to stay away from strangers. We need to establish who are friends and who are enemies … and why."

"You know what your mom would say, don't you?" Mark asks, smiling.

"Yes," I answer, "she would say that those feelings are from the Holy Spirit and that God is with us. God is guiding us by giving us those feelings."

"Well, don't argue with the Holy Spirit," Dad says. "God has given us a safe place. We will just stay put and not move around today. But I do think we need to make contact with someone we know."

"Does anyone come to mind?" I ask.

"It needs to be someone mature, someone the officials wouldn't think to question. Someone who doesn't engage in gossip or believe every story told about someone."

"If we need someone who is mature and not easily rattled, I know just the person!" I say excitedly. "Mrs. Felder is mature. She should be; she's ninety. I've been going by and visiting with her every week, sometimes more often than that. She has never stopped praying for me and for you and Mom. She is a true servant of the Lord. She is someone not many outsiders would know is a friend. Dad, what do you think?"

"I think she would be perfect," Dad says. "But I think if we both have this fear of what these strangers might do, we should pray about it first. We could be bringing harm to her doorstep just by contacting her." Mark begins quoting from the Bible, and before the second word, I join him, and we complete the verses together.

"If any of you lacks wisdom, you should ask God, who gives generously to all without finding fault, and it will be given to you. But when you ask, you must believe and not doubt, because the one who doubts is like a wave of the sea, blown and tossed by the wind" (James 1:5-6).

"Dad, I feel like Mrs. Felder is the one to go to. How about you?"

"Yes, I feel the same way. We can at least get food and maybe some news from her."

We drink from the spring and re-bandage our wounds. We rest, nap, and wait for evening, when we can start off for the Felder place. It is northeast of us, not far "as the crow flies." We'll have to zigzag, following the terrain.

Mr. Felder died several years ago, and Dad promised to check in on Mrs. Felder. I remember in junior high I would ride over on Chesterfield. Mrs. Felder always had cookies and lemonade ready. When I got my license to drive, I visited less frequently—until I stopped going altogether my senior year. I started back a year ago, about a month after Mom's funeral.

Mr. and Mrs. Felder never owned the mineral rights to their ranch. Their only income was from the ranch, and they barely made ends meet. They were frugal and got by somehow. They didn't have any kids, but they spoiled me and lots of neighbor children over the years. Mrs. Felder helped us when my mom got sick, bringing meals over to the house, always taking time to pray with us before she left. She is what you would call a "prayer warrior." I'm sure her prayers saw me through my withdrawal from drugs upon returning to the ranch. She always prayed with me before I left her place, prayers that were sincere, full of love and respect for God and for His power. She prayed the way some people carry on a conversation. I always felt a renewed strength on my way home, as if I could make it through the day and night after visiting her. She is definitely a friend who can be trusted.

We have a clear night with a moon that is half full. It's not so light that we will be seen easily, yet we can see to go where we need to go. After the rain, everything has more dimensions. The colors are more defined, from dark cedar-greens to lighter sage-greens. Some of the bushes in the bottoms even have reddish hues to them. These colors make eerie shadows in the night. When the dusty caliche powder covers everything, all vegetation is pretty much the same.

We make pretty good time through the night. We jog where we can and avoid talking. We only stop when necessary, pushing ourselves. The days are shorter now, so we are able to travel almost a full ten hours before stopping in a creek bottom not far from Mrs. Felder's. We should make it to her house tomorrow, for sure.

We rest and sleep in the shade of the trees most of the day. About two o'clock we get up and think about something to eat, but it will have to wait. The helicopter is in the sky again. We know we shouldn't move during the day. If the wildlife spooks, it could give our position away, and we have nowhere to hide.

"Let's talk about that night and everything we can remember," Dad says.

Not That Bruce Willis!

"That's probably a good idea," I say, "because they'll want us to tell them what happened when we can talk to the sheriff. Is Sheriff Taylor still there?"

"Yes," Dad says, "and I'm sure if we could get to him, he would believe us and help us out. I consider him a good Christian friend."

We recount to each other our experiences of that night as we walk. We keep to the protection of the trees, because there is still a helicopter somewhere overhead. We travel in the roughest and deepest ravines, because we can't be seen from the roads. It takes longer than we expect to get to the barn and small farmhouse. It is nearly dark and our stomachs are growling.

A deputy's truck is in the drive. We hide close to the back of the house. We peek inside to see if the deputy is Doug. Dad and Doug were in the same grade in school, and he is sure Doug will help. About that time, the back door opens, and the new deputy emerges from the back door carrying a tray of sandwiches, cookies, and all the fixings. The sight of the food makes us even hungrier. We pray that our stomachs wouldn't growl as we sink back further into the shadows.

It seems strange that this deputy would be here so late at night. Perhaps he knows of the Willis' friendship with the old woman. Maybe there is news, and they can come out of hiding.

Mrs. Felder comes out onto the back patio carrying their drinks. She is not happy about something; I can tell by her expression. They both step back inside the house for a minute. We move around to where we can be close enough to help her if trouble breaks out. We don't trust this stranger. We are also close enough to hear them talking.

"Young man," Mrs. Felder says firmly, "you have been here all afternoon trying to poison my mind against my neighbors. You don't know them. I do! You don't know what you're talking about. Bruce wouldn't hurt a fly. And I don't know what I would've done without Mark Willis helping me after my husband died."

"Well," says the deputy, "we found evidence of a drug deal. There were drugs—illegal drugs, the kind the kid used in college—a little money, and three unidentified men dead. They were shot with a rifle, the same caliber as Bruce's. Caliber means the same size of bullet. Bruce's rifle is missing, and so is his dad. We think he's killed his dad and that we'll find his remains one day in the canyons. We are positive the boy is dangerous. We want you to call us immediately if you see or hear from him. Do you understand?" He says everything loudly and slowly, as if he is talking to a feeble-minded, old woman for whom he has little or no respect.

"I think you're mistaken," she starts to say but is immediately cut off.

"Old lady, I don't think you understand," the deputy says. "These are bad men. You live a long, long way from anyone. No one would find your dead, rotting body for days. Who knows? You could be next. Do I make myself clear? Call us if you see or hear from them. They are dangerous." He stares at her, getting right in her face, sneering when he's finished. He moves over slowly and takes hold of Mrs. Felder's shoulders. "Mrs. Felder, you remind me of that little old lady in the Sylvester and Tweety cartoons. You feel as small and frail as she looked. Don't you realize that none of us knows what happened? The same thing could happen to you, *right here and now*. You *are* alone. No one knows when a stranger might come by. You need to beware, and watch your mouth! You might want to tell us if you hear or see anything out of the ordinary—or else I can't protect you." The threat is clear, and he smiles and hugs her in a confining way.

The thinly-veiled threat is not lost on Mrs. Felder. I see the change in her posture and hear her immediately change her tune. She speaks in a weak, frail voice that doesn't even sound like her. "Do you think they would harm me?" she asks. She fusses with the little, white-haired bun on top of her head. I start to stand, and my dad puts his hand on my shoulder.

"Now you understand the danger," he says. "Yes, they will harm you. Don't talk to them. Don't let them even see you. You just call us if you see them." He smiles as if his mission is accomplished.

"Oh, Officer, I just didn't understand. I will! I most definitely will! I will call you and keep my doors locked. Thank you for coming out to warn me. You know, I don't feel safe anymore. Who knows what evil is lurking near." She looks wide-eyed and frightened.

"Oh, don't worry," the deputy threatens. "I'll stay with you until I'm sure you understand the danger you face."

"I understand. I'm going to bed early. I just don't feel good." Mrs. Felder grabs the platter of food and dumps it in the dog's bowl before the deputy has a chance to fill his plate. "Goodnight," she says. And she is gone.

Upstairs, Mrs. Felder turns a light on and looks out across the now-dark night. She continues to scan the horizon as if she is looking for something or someone. I see her cross the room to her bedroom door, lock it, and put a chair under the doorknob. She goes back to the window, sits down on her bed fully clothed, and weeps. Watching all of this makes my blood boil. Whoever this man is, I want to throttle him!

Does she know we are here? Does she fear us or the deputy? Maybe she trusts no one now. We decide to stay up and watch over her tonight, to make sure she is safe. If we need to help her, we will use our bare hands if we have to. We definitely won't approach her at night. We'll wait until morning.

The deputy goes to his truck, but he doesn't leave. Dad keeps an eye on the deputy as I creep up to the back patio and scoop the sandwiches and cookies into my backpack. I know that Mrs. Felder's dog died over a month ago. Why has she put the food in his bowl? Just out of habit, I guess. What the deputy has said to her would rattle anyone. We retreat up the canyon wall where we can see Mrs. Felder's window and the deputy's truck. We are far enough away that we risk a few whispers to each other as we devour the sandwiches.

"Well, there is our friend," I say.

"And there is our enemy," Dad adds.

Interlude

Great Performance Theater

Sheriff Taylor looks around and finds evidence that this fire was started by someone. He calls a friend at the fire marshal's office and asks him to check it out discreetly.

Chapter 9 - Mrs. Felder

The morning dawns with Deputy Lowe still at the Felder home. Dad and I have taken turns watching over Mrs. Felder through the night. Everything is calm, and we have moved back to our hidden position from the night before. Mrs. Felder is bustling about the kitchen, fixing breakfast. She comes outside to throw some potato peels away. She glances at the dog's bowl and goes back inside. She doesn't acknowledge that it is empty.

Deputy Lowe begins to set the table outside. We're sure he has been instructed to do so by Mrs. Felder. She has a way of asking you to do something so that you know your only choice is to answer, "Yes, ma'am." She carries out a large platter of bacon, sausage links, eggs, and hash browns. Deputy Lowe brings out the biscuits and gravy. They sit down to eat, and this time the deputy digs in before she feeds it to the dog. When his plate is as full as he can get it, he asks, "Mrs. Felder, do you normally fix this much food?"

Mrs. Felder smiles and bats her fading brown eyes and says, "Oh, Deputy Lowe, you just don't know how nice it is to have someone look out for me. Not since my Emil left me several years ago have I felt so safe. Are you married, Deputy Lowe? Do you have a family, a son perhaps? Let me get you more coffee." She refills his cup, not waiting for an answer. For herself, she eats only a small bowl of oatmeal.

He has a puzzled look on his face. "Mrs. Felder, this is just an official visit, and I am not married," he says with a mouthful of food. "I am trying to make sure that you and your neighbors realize that the Willises cannot be trusted. I believe completely that even if Mark Willis is alive, he would say anything to protect his son."

Not That Bruce Willis!

"I'm sure you're right. Well, I guess I just didn't want you to go away hungry, and quite truthfully, I forgot how much a man can eat. Please have some more if you would like. It must be a dreadfully lonely profession you are in. A life without family is terribly lonely." She refills his coffee again, emphasizing the word *lonely*.

Deputy Lowe seems bored with the conversation. "I will need to be on my way this morning to the next house. I believe you understand the seriousness now. I am glad that you do. I would sure hate for anything to happen to you." He gave her a deadly serious stare.

Mrs. Felder's eyes snap, but she keeps her composure. She sweetly smiles back at him as if he has given her a compliment for all of the breakfast she prepared. I wonder what she might have up her sleeve. Then she changes the subject while pouring Deputy Lowe yet more coffee. "Mr. Lowe, I mean, Deputy Lowe, may we talk about some other subject? You are frightening an old woman, and I do not want to run into the house and spend the entire day indoors just yet. That would be almost as lonely as you must be, driving around, trying to protect everyone, *all by your lonesome.*" She said it ever so politely, slowing down to emphasize the last words.

"Sure. Whatever," he says, shoveling in food without looking up. Mrs. Felder makes sure his coffee cup is as full as his mouth.

Dad and I can tell she is about to blow her top. She seldom gets angry, but when she does, she is passionate. She takes a breath to calm down and says, "What is your favorite movie of all time?"

"I dun-no," he mumbles while finishing the last of his coffee. She refills his cup again as he begins to round up his hat and keys.

She fills a large Styrofoam coffee cup and smiles with a twinkle in her eye. "This coffee is for the road," she says. "And by the way, my favorite movie is one with Cary Grant. Don't you just love Cary Grant? I do. He was quite the lady's man back in my day. One of his early films was a comedy entitled *Arsenic and Old Lace*. Have you heard of it?"

He shakes his head no and takes a big drink of coffee. She tops it off.

"Oh, let me tell you about it!" she says, clapping her hands together and putting them very ladylike in her lap.

"Sure," he grumps, standing to put on his hat and coat.

"Mortimer—that is, Cary Grant—has just gotten married, and he has to tell his two maiden, elderly aunts that he is married and leaving them. He discovers, however, that they are touched in the head. You know, crazy?" She waits for a response.

"Yeah, sure," he mumbles, rolling his eyes. He slowly walks around the house toward his pickup, barely looking at the old woman as she accompanies him, prattling on.

"Mortimer discovers that his aunts have a pastime of killing lonely old men by putting arsenic in their wine and burying them in the basement." She giggles a bit, as if she remembers a line from the movie. "Mortimer thinks that maybe insanity runs in the family. He wonders how he will break that news to his new wife. The way they hide the bodies is so funny. Oh, well, you just need to rent it sometime. I think you will find it interesting, a smart man like you." This time, she is the one to lock stares with Deputy Lowe. At that point, it apparently sinks in that he is the only one drinking coffee, and lots of it.

Deputy Lowe doesn't wait to say good-bye. He throws the rest of his coffee away, gets in his truck, and speeds off.

Mrs. Felder waves goodbye, smiling and humming the *Death March* as she returns to the house.

Dad and I look at each other, shocked!

"Oh, boys, you can come out now! He's gone!" Mrs. Felder calls out as she rounds the corner of the house to the back patio.

Dad and I slowly come out of the bushes to approach the patio.

Mrs. Felder claps her hands like a little girl. She is beaming and trots forward to greet us with a hug. "Praise God! I have been praying that you two were all right. I just felt like you were close last night. This morning when the food was gone, I knew for sure. Come, eat, and tell me all about what's happened." She walks back to the patio table with us.

"No coffee for me, Mrs. Felder," Dad says with a smile. "Thank you, though." And Mrs. Felder doubles over in laughter.

"Tell me; you didn't really poison him did you?" I ask, more than a little worried about my favorite neighbor. She is like my adopted grandma.

"No, dear child. I would never do anything like that. However, a few of my senna leaves may have gotten into the coffee grounds and brewed with the coffee. How dare he threaten me! Doesn't he know that the only thing this ninety-year-old has to look forward to *is* death? He's going to wonder for a while, though, whether he has been poisoned or not. I hope he makes it back to town before he has to go to the bathroom." She begins to chuckle uncontrollably. The genuine laughter is contagious, and soon we are all laughing. Of course, I have no idea about what.

"Mrs. Felder, what are senna leaves?" I catch my breath long enough to ask the question.

"Sweety, it is one of nature's laxatives. As much as Deputy Lowe drank, I'd say he should be clean as a whistle by tomorrow." Laughter erupts from everyone, now that we are all in on the joke. We begin to eat. I feel like God has led us here, and I feel very safe in this ninety-year-old woman's home.

Interlude

Intersection of Highways 60 and 83

Sheriff Taylor has been examining the scene of the overturned truck. He goes to the lot where the wrecked truck has been taken and finds that it has been removed. There is no record of who picked it up or when they came for it.

Chapter 10 - Waiting

We devour the rest of breakfast, filling Mrs. Felder in on what has happened and our suspicions about the deputy.

We decide that when Deputy Lowe is better, he will definitely be back for revenge, and that Mrs. Felder should go to Amarillo and stay with her sister. She is younger, but not by much, and just as fearless as Mrs. Felder. Her son, Mrs. Felder's nephew, is sixty and has been in the FBI for forty years. He holds a highly respected position, and Mrs. Felder is sure he will be able to help.

Mrs. Felder's niece lives next door and has three grandsons staying with her while they go to college. They should be able to provide enough protection if the deputy follows her to Amarillo. We help her pack her things into her older-model Buick. She says she will go out by way of the back roads and avoid Canadian.

We trade cell phones with Mrs. Felder. That way she will have one in case of emergency, but it won't otherwise be used—in case our phone is being monitored for activity. She will have her nephew call us tonight at ten. She tells us that her cell phone is fully charged and nearly brand new, so it should last for a long time if we leave it off when we're not using it. She gives us the charger anyway, just in case. The only problem will be finding somewhere safe to charge it, but we'll cross that bridge when we come to it.

Mrs. Felder tells us to take whatever we need from the house and gives us nearly a hundred dollars. She says she has a credit card she never uses, so this will give her a chance to earn some points. When she turns those fading, soulful eyes upon us, we take the money reluctantly. We might need it, and we can't very well go to the bank or use our credit or debit cards. The officials would know immediately where we are and narrow their search. I sure hope it isn't long before we clear this mess up, but it feels like it might never be resolved.

Before driving away, she writes a note to the mailman and pins it on the outside of the front door. It reads: Buster, I am too afraid to stay here alone. I have gone to a motel. Keep my mail at the post office. I will pick it up there. Thanks, Isabelle. The note is more for Deputy Lowe if he returns than for the mailman.

Together, Dad and I gather some food, coffee, a couple of blankets, and a canteen. He checks the charge on the cell phone while I look for some twenty-two-caliber bullets for my pistol. I find some in a back closet. Dad notices a newspaper that the deputy must have brought to the house, and we take it to read later. We straighten everything up after packing and lock the doors.

As we're leaving, we see the washhouse and stop to look in the window. We see all of Emil's clothes hanging against the back wall. We grab a couple of jackets and coveralls, because the evenings will be getting cooler. We shouldn't be hiding for too much longer with the FBI looking into the strange events. But neither Dad nor I can see an end in sight. We may be on the run for quite a while.

Emil kept his twenty-two rifle in the washhouse too, so we take it, along with more shells. We pick up propane lighters, an old coffee pot we can set on a fire, an old towel, a small skillet, two tin pie pans, two spoons, and two forks. We use the blankets to bundle our supplies. I wear my own backpack in front and carry the blanket pack over my back.

We begin our trip back to the cave before dark this time, but we stay in the ravine, out of sight. By dark, we are a third of the way back. Walking all night, we arrive at the cave in the early hours of the morning. We are on top of the ridge. Dropping our packs and hopping down to the ledge, we realize that something is not right. Someone has been here.

"Dad, look," I say. "These twigs on this bush are broken, and there's a place where someone or something has slid a little. It couldn't have been us, because we didn't come up that way when we were here before." I scan the horizon with an awful feeling that we aren't alone anymore.

The day ends with the moon sliding silently across the clear, star-filled sky. Ten o'clock comes, and there's no phone call. We check the reception, and it shows three bars. Finally, at fifteen minutes after ten, the cell phone rings. Dad picks up, and flips the phone on speaker phone. The man's voice on the other end is loud enough that they can both hear it.

"This is Ted Newton," says a voice on the other end. "I am Isabelle Felder's nephew."

"This is Mark Willis," says Dad. "We are so glad to hear from you. Did Mrs. Felder fill you in on what has happened out here?"

"Yes. But I would like for you to tell me."

"It was Friday night of last week," Dad says. "My son Bruce stays at the ranch, and I stay at the office in an efficiency apartment upstairs. The trouble started at the ranch, so I'll let Bruce tell you how the evening began." Dad hands the phone to me.

I begin my story, telling Mr. Newton everything that happened the night the intruders came, and everything that Dad and I have been discussing and puzzling over for the past few days.

I hand the phone back to Dad.

My dad jumps in with his own account and then adds, "I just remembered something else from the Denali ride. These men were not working alone. In the car, they took a call and said that they had me and that it would soon be over. They would call back as soon as it was finished."

"Thank you, for filling me in," Ted Newton says. "If you should think of something you failed to mention, write it down so you'll remember to tell me the next time we talk. I'll call again tomorrow at the same time. Until then, I'll see what I can come up with. Are you safe where you are?"

"Yes, we think so," Dad tells him. "It seems like someone has been here, but no one has come back."

Not That Bruce Willis!

"I want you to assume that it is not safe," Ted says. "Can you observe this place from a distance and watch to see if someone comes?"

"Yes, we can," Dad says, "but do you really think that's necessary?"

"Absolutely," Ted answers. "If someone gets to you two, we may never unravel what is really happening. Trust no one. Call no one. Stay out of sight, and don't move around. Wait for me to see what I can come up with, okay?"

"Okay," Dad says. We'll move now and will talk to you tomorrow at ten p.m. Ted, thanks." Dad spoke with emotion in his voice.

We move silently in the dark to the opposite rim of the ravine, where can see the cave and anyone approaching it. Dad will take the first watch while I try to sleep. Since we can't build a fire, we sit with our backs to the rocks, wrapped up in the blankets, and wait.

Interlude

Motel in Colorado

Sheriff Taylor takes a trip to Colorado while he is not needed in his town. He checks into a small motel, immediately gets on the Internet, and begins to search. He finds the phone numbers of the agencies he is looking for and writes them down. He lays his cell phone down and picks up the motel phone.

Chapter 11 - Martha

A week has passed, and Ted Newton is still digging for information during the day and calling Mark Willis at night. He's trying to make inquiries without anyone knowing who he is or that he is with the FBI. He tells people he is a reporter and shares with them what he has found out so far. He has been allowed on the ranch to see where the deaths took place. He sees how all of Bruce's claims can be proven.

There is the bullet hole in the apple tree. If there were no guns on the strangers, who shot at the tree? A farmer who was working cattle early Saturday morning saw a wrecker towing a fancy black SUV down the road. He remembers it because he thought to himself that his old farm truck would outlast any new vehicle. Ted checks the neighboring towns, asking if someone has had a gas tank cleaned recently. A black Denali with sugar in the gas tank was taken into a garage in Wheeler the day after the attack. The repair was paid for with cash, and the attendant didn't know who owned the car.

The next time Ted Newton calls, he has some new questions for Dad and me.

"Mark," Ted asks, "can you tell me if I can trust the Sheriff Taylor? Realize that you are betting your life and Bruce's on this man if you say yes."

"Yes," Dad tells him confidently, "I believe he is someone you can trust. He's a deacon at the church with me. We grew up together, and I think if anyone knows the truth about us, it would be him."

"Then I'll talk to him tomorrow and call you tomorrow night," Ted says.

Not That Bruce Willis!

We haven't seen anyone for three days, including helicopters, but we decide that if we do see anyone, we'll high-tail it out of there and not look back. Saturday morning catches us off guard. First, we notice the movement of birds taking flight. Then, we hear the snapping of twigs underfoot. Instead of leaving as we swore we would, we stay to see what or who is here.

It's someone wearing camouflage, but he appears unarmed. He walks straight up to the cave, as if he knows exactly where he is going. He doesn't have a gun, so he isn't a hunter. He approaches from the same side where we saw the broken twigs and slide marks.

"Who knows about this place?" I whisper.

"No one," Dad whispers back. "That is, no one living. Only my Dad and I ever came here. He made me promise not to tell a soul. Because of the petroglyphs on the walls, he didn't want tourists to spoil this one remaining refuge on our ranch."

The stranger walks out from behind the cedar in front of the cave and looks around. It is a woman! Dad begins to make his way down the ravine into the bottom. I don't know where he is going, but I follow him. He walks up the creek toward the cave as the woman comes down from it.

"Martha?" both of us say at the same time.

"Mark! Bruce!" Martha says, almost sobbing. "I'm so thankful to find you!"

They meet at the bottom of the trail, and Dad rushes to embrace her. I stand back a bit. I have never really liked Aunt Martha. She may be Dad's twin sister, but she is nothing like him. She is cool and calculating, acting one way in front of Dad and another when he is out of sight. I have seen her tell lies without batting an eye. I remember reading the headlines a few years ago, and I believe every word of them—except the part that said Aunt Martha knew nothing about her husband's illegal dealings.

When I think of what I remember about Aunt Martha and Uncle Harold, I am swept back to that time. He was a Wall Street investment broker, sought after by the rich and famous to do their investing for them. He also had many well-educated families investing with him because he was so good. These families managed to save back and put away funds for their retirement—only to find out one day that all of their investment was gone. At age sixty-five, they had to get jobs in order to keep their homes. The rich and famous had many charities they were responsible for, and they discovered that those charities were bankrupt. Uncle Harold stole from orphanages and churches. There were no funds to cover thousands of clients' monies. And the theft went on for years.

My uncle pled no contest and went to prison. He had off-shore accounts that the government couldn't touch. He had a mistress and an illegitimate son who were living in the Cayman Islands in a plush mansion. The government seized all of the property and assets stateside. My aunt and uncle had been living the high life for decades. Aunt Martha was left homeless and penniless, but she escaped imprisonment, because they couldn't prove that she knew anything.

I take a step back from her as I relive all of this in my mind again. She turns to me with sincerity, holding out her arms to embrace me also. I allow her a short hug.

"Mark, little Brucie has grown so much since I last saw you. I'm so glad to see you both alive and well. The newspapers had you both dead." She smiles and continues. "I am sorry about missing Theresa's funeral. I was out of the country. That's why you couldn't reach me. I'm so sorry; I got so wrapped up in my own life's trials that I didn't even make contact with you this past year. I was trying to line up some exports for our beef." She has said all this without making eye contact. "I do appreciate the house and the job, by the way," she goes on. "I don't think I ever told you. It has been a life-line for me." She rattles on so fast that neither Dad nor I can get a word in edgewise. She finally takes a breath, and Dad speaks.

"Martha, you could have called," Dad said with disappointment. "You knew Theresa was ill. I know you two never saw eye-to-eye, but you could have at least called for my sake."

Not That Bruce Willis!

Dad and I knew Martha was out of the country, but it wasn't for business. She was trying to pressure her husband's mistress into giving her the house in the Cayman Islands.

Martha had resented Dad ever since their mother had passed away when they were teenagers. It was obvious that she resented working and having to live in a house Dad bought for her. She believed that their parents' will had been changed to give her half of everything. When she found out it hadn't and that Dad was to inherit everything, she acted like it was his fault.

Even my dad thought that their father had changed the will to include Martha. I heard him tell my mom that Grandpa was tired of arguing with Martha and was going to the lawyer to make some changes, and Dad believed Martha had won. In fact, just before Grandpa died in a car wreck, Dad told his sister so. After Grandpa's death, it became clear that his visit to the lawyer was for the purpose of making the will ironclad. Knowing the situation gave me an insight into my Dad's relationship with his twin sister.

"I know, Mark," Martha is saying. "I'm sorry." Then she turns to me and changes the subject. "Bruce you look quite well." She says it almost as if she is surprised I'm not drunk or higher than a kite.

I know she expects to see me strung out on drugs. *People who live in glass houses shouldn't throw stones*, I hear my mom's voice say in my head. "Thank you, Aunt Martha," I say. "You look like you have recovered well, too." Two can play this game of innuendoes.

"Forget the formalities, Martha," Dad says. "What are you doing here? Did anyone follow you?"

"I read in the papers what happened. I came immediately. I've set up shop in the office here to run both the feed lot and the processing plant in Nebraska. I knew you would find your way here if you were alive and needed a place to hide. As for your other question, I don't think anyone followed me. It would be rather obvious on these flat mesas. Besides, why don't you give yourselves up to the police?" Martha sounds offended.

"We can't trust them," Dad tells her. "They're trying to shoot us."

I'm thinking that Martha has a strange way of putting things. Instead of saying, "Why don't you ask the police for help?" she says, "give yourselves up." And she mentions us coming to the cave if we need a place to hide. Why would she think that we need to hide ... and from whom?

Martha looks at our duffle bag and says she sees that we must've snuck back to the house to get a few supplies. She asks if we need anything, like a gun or food? I wonder if she asks about the gun just to see if we have one. Dad tells her that we have a hand gun and food. I wish my dad would not be so forthcoming about what we have or don't have. Neither of us tells her about Mrs. Felder; something tells us to keep that to ourselves. We are still in a very protective mode of thinking when it comes to Mrs. Felder. Besides, it isn't important where we got our supplies.

I think about of the movie The Sixth Sense with Bruce Willis. I remember his character, Dr. Crowe finds that the mother is the one to give her daughter the poison. I feel our danger is someone close to us too. I don't like what I'm thinking. I have to remind myself that I'm not that Bruce Willis. I don't trust Martha. I've seen the devastation of Martha's and Harold's Ponzi scheme, what it has done to orphanages, missions, and other charitable organizations. Harold fooled many people. No one ever proved that Martha knew of his scheme, but I believe she did. I know my dad is blind when it comes to Martha. I can see her expressions when my father isn't looking. It seems like she is always putting on an act whenever he's around. Sometimes I wonder if she hypnotizes him.

Mark looks at his sister and feels sorry for her all over again. She was his elder by two minutes, so technically she is the firstborn. Their mother died of a sudden heart attack when they were sixteen. Their father was a strict taskmaster. He believed that men should work hard, and women should marry well. After his wife's death, he rewrote his will to reflect his beliefs. In his will, he left everything—land, house, equipment, business, and mineral rights—to Mark. He also got the guns and farm and ranch heirlooms.

Not That Bruce Willis!

Martha, even though she was the older of the two, was to receive her mother's personal belongings—jewelry, domestic items, furniture, piano, china, any and all heirloom items that were of a feminine nature—and a one-hundred-thousand-dollar dowry.

Their father thought he was protecting Martha by making sure that any man who would marry his little girl would be marrying her for love and not money. Mark and his sister always believed she would share equally in the millions of Willard Willis, rancher and oil tycoon. It was when Martha met and married a smart New York graduate that they found out differently.

Harold had a very bright and promising future in marketing. He was a natural for Wall Street. When they married, they found out about the dowry. But they still didn't know how her father's assets would be split upon his death. It didn't take long to find out. The same year that Martha married, Willard Willis died in a freak car wreck. He ran off a curve and landed in a steep canyon. The will was read, and that was when they found out that Mark owned everything. There were even special stipulations on the property. Mark could not give or sell any of the property to anyone. He was to retain ownership in order to keep it. If he didn't, it would be liquidated and given to specified charities. He was to remain sole owner, and everything was to be passed to the next male or males in the family. Should there be no males, then and only then would the legacy pass to the nearest living female.

Martha and Harold flourished. Harold was an expert at separating people from their money. He had three fabulous estates in the United States and one in the Caribbean. The Caribbean property was more modest, and Martha never liked going there. It was mainly an escape for Harold. Martha used the other homes in the United States for entertaining the rich and famous. Everything was wonderful, until the stock market crashed.

Then the truth came out. Harold had only been trading things on paper and doctoring the books so that it showed fabulous gains for his clients. He took all of their money and put it into his own assets. When someone asked for proof or money, he would produce the paperwork or even move enough money to pay them. It wasn't until everyone wanted their money all at once that the truth came out. He couldn't pay everyone, because the money wasn't there.

The government seized all of his assets and homes in the United States. They couldn't touch the offshore accounts and the Caribbean home. Harold had deeded that property a long time ago to his mistress. He made sure it was rock solid and that no one could ever touch it. There was also an account set up in her name that couldn't be touched. She had an illegitimate son by him. Paternity tests proved this to be true. His idea of honor was to financially provide for her and the boy. Harold went to jail and refused to cooperate with the government.

Martha, on the other hand, was left to deal with the mess. She had no assets of her own—not even a home—because they were all in joint ownership. It could never be proven that she had prior knowledge of her husband's business dealings. Mark gave her a job at the Nebraska office of the Willis Cattle Company. She managed the feed lots for the north central region. She made a handsome salary, and he gave her a half-million-dollar home to live in, with all bills paid by the company. She took it and acted appreciative.

"Earth to Mark," Martha says, interrupting her brother's thoughts. "What on earth were you thinking about?"

"I was just thinking about you," Mark answers. "Why did you come all the way out here?"

"I love you. Isn't that enough of a reason?" Martha says this with such sincerity that even I feel bad for doubting her. "Mark, what can I do?" she asks. "Seriously, what is happening?"

We invite her to share our campfire and a cup of coffee. We tell her everything we know. Dad doesn't tell her about Ted Newton; I wonder why, but I don't ask. Martha says she should get back to the office before anyone notices she's gone. She will tell Sheriff Taylor the truth and see if they can figure out a way to protect us and clear Dad's name. We warn her not to talk to Deputy Lowe or anyone else—male or female—that she doesn't positively know. She is to trust only the Sheriff Taylor. She starts off at a brisk pace and is soon out of sight.

Interlude

Motel in Colorado

The phone rings in a small motel in the foothills of the Rockies.

"This is Sheriff Taylor. Who is calling, please."

"That isn't important. Can I talk to you about the missing Willis men?"

"Who is this?"

"I can't tell you over the phone. I will meet you at your favorite fishing hole. You told my uncle about it. I will be there within the hour."

The call ends, and the sheriff checks his gun, puts on his hat and coat, and leaves the room.

Chapter 12 - Revelations

Dad is quiet, almost like he is in mourning. I'm nervous. I ask my dad why he didn't mention Ted Newton to Aunt Martha. He says he just thought it might make Ted's job harder somehow. The way he says this, it's like he regrets something. I'm so uneasy my skin is crawling. I mention it to Dad.

"Dad, I think someone might have followed Aunt Martha. I think we should stuff some of Emil's clothes and put them just inside the cave, as if we were sitting there. Then we should hide somewhere and watch. I can just feel the danger. What do you think?" I ask.

"If someone followed her, he would have already made his move," Dad answers in a husky voice. "He would have shot all of us, including Martha."

"I agree," I say as I stuff a shirt with leaves," but it's better to be safe than sorry."

In no time, we have two figures in the shadows of the cave. We literally run away from the cave as if it might explode. Just as we reach an outcropping of rocks, Deputy Lowe shows up with two men. They creep up on the cave. They know exactly where it is and move in close. Deputy Lowe is carrying my rifle. He aims and fires, blowing the leaf man over. Then there's another shot, but Dad and I are long gone. We are running down the creek, heading for a small lake on Wolf Creek. It's getting late in the season, but maybe we can find somewhere to hide or someone to help us until we can talk to Ted at ten o'clock. We need somewhere safe to stop and wait for Ted's call.

Is this our Armageddon? We are facing overwhelming odds and unknown dangers. Bruce Willis' character in that movie is Harry

Not That Bruce Willis!

Stamper, the hero. I know I'm no hero, but then I'm not that Bruce Willis.

"Bruce," Dad says between heavy breaths, "if we don't feel safe when we get to the lake, I think we should use Mrs. Felder's money and hitch a ride toward the Rockies."

I'm not quite as winded as he is. "Sure, Dad," I respond. "I don't think it is safe around here anymore, either. Maybe Ted will call with some answers. We'll need to clean up a little. We're looking a little rough around the edges. If we approach someone the way we look now, it could scare them."

We are both ready to go off the grid and disappear. We'll make our way toward the Rockies and hope to be swallowed up by the mountains, if need be. We need to find someone with out-of-state tags. Maybe they aren't interested in local news and won't have heard about us. I hope that the news about us has died down by now. We'll have to make up some story as to why we don't have any travel bags with us.

We keep running through the night, staying away from roads whenever we can. Our phone doesn't have any reception at ten o'clock—or all night, for that matter. When we see the storm clouds building again, we thank God for the rain that will wash away our tracks. At dawn we stop running and hide in a grove of cottonwoods where a pond once stood during wetter weather. The rain was brief, but it was enough to wash away all traces of which way we went. We lie down and the phone rings. It is five o'clock in the morning. We wonder if we should answer it, but it seems necessary. If it isn't Ted, we'll hang up immediately. The phone remains on speaker phone. "Hello," Dad says.

"Where have you been?" Ted asks. "What's happened? I've called every hour, on the hour, all night long."

"We're okay for the moment," Dad tells him. "We had to run. The deputy found the cave and brought two other men with him. He shot what he thought was us, but it was some clothes we stuffed. We ran all night and didn't stop until just a moment ago."

"Are you safe?" Ted asks.

"Yes. We don't think anyone followed us. The rain helped by washing away our tracks."

Interrupting, Ted says, "Don't tell me where you are. I'm not sure your phone is safe anymore. There have been major compromises within the system. The only way this could've happened is with a lot of money. What I do know is that someone wants you dead—someone who will stop at nothing. Do you have any ideas who this might be? I need a lead. They're getting closer to you than I am to them. Think hard and tell me anyone who would benefit from your death, anyone that you may have made angry."

Dad takes a deep breath, looks to the heavens and a clear blue sky, and says a prayer. "Lord, let me be right. Please don't let me be blinded anymore. Show me, sweet Jesus, what I must see, and give me the words I must say."

"Mark," Ted shouts, "are you there? Did you hear me? Answer me."

Dad moves away from me and answers. "Yes, I'm here. My twin sister is the one who will benefit from my death. Her name is Martha Weinstein, Mrs. Harold Weinstein. Before you ask, yes, she's that Martha Weinstein from the Wall Street scandal. That was her husband, but I doubt he did all of those things alone. Martha has a super-high IQ and an overpowering need to rule everyone and everything around her. She came to the camp today. It wasn't very long after she left that the deputy showed up with his buddies. She's the only one who knew about the cave besides my father and my son. These men knew exactly where to go. After Theresa died, I changed my will to leave everything to Bruce; but in the event that Bruce was also gone, it would all go to Martha. She is very dangerous. I see that now for the first time in my life. She is capable of anything. Talk to my lawyer, Sam Bradford. He can fill you in on our families sorted past as it pertains to finances. Don't approach Martha directly, Ted. I don't know what she is capable of doing, and I still love her," Dad says, visibly shaken. "Ted, please prove my suspicions to be wrong. But either way thank you for helping us."

"Mark," says Ted, "this may be the piece of the puzzle I need. I'll tell you more later. Do you have anything else you can remember about Martha? I need to know all of your suspicions."

Not That Bruce Willis!

"There is one more person I want you to look into, her name is Cindy Monroe. She came into my son's life just as Martha's life was falling apart from the scandal." Dad replies and adds. "Bruce and I will talk and get back to you if we think of anything that might help."

They say their good byes and hang up. Dad sits down and I join him. I wait for him to talk. Once dad speaks it is like he is traveling back in time re-living his childhood.

"Martha was more ambitious and aggressive than I. I would rather make peace than argue. Martha, on the other hand, thrived on chaos. She was spoiled. We both were, because our parents could afford to spoil us. Our parents gave her whatever she wanted … well, almost. She would get others to do her dirty work, including me. I never told my parents about the pranks she pulled at school. She was wise beyond her years." Dad began.

"What kind of pranks?" I ask not really knowing what to say. I can tell dad needs to unburden himself, but it makes me feel funny to hear all of this.

"In fourth grade, there was a bully who would stop us when we walked to the feedlot office after school. He had a big pit bull, and he demanded money each time. The boy was older and bigger than us. I was scared to death, but not Martha. She loved to be in power.

"After about a week of these shakedowns, Martha said it would end that day. When the boy showed up, Martha told him to leave us alone, that she had told her dad about him, and he was going to sue the boy's father. The boy laughed and said that they had nothing and to go ahead. He told his dog to get us, and Martha pulled out a chunk of roast from her pocket. She threw it toward the dog, but instead of running, she waited for it to eat the meat, smiling as she watched. I remember. She seemed to enjoy it. When the dog was finished, its mouth began to foam. It couldn't breathe. The boy shrieked that she had killed his dog. He cradled his dog and cried like a baby. I asked Martha what she put in the meat. She smiled sweetly and said, "Rat poison."

"We found out later that the dog was all the boy had in this world. He didn't have any family. He was homeless and had made friends with the dog. So I guess the dog was his family. I told Martha what I had found out and that I felt bad for him. We had so much, and he had nothing. Martha got up in my face and told me never to show weakness around her again. Power is in the pain, she said. I didn't understand that statement then, but I do now." Dad says.

"Can you remember anything else that makes you think that Martha is involved in what is happening to us now?" I ask.

"When I think back, I realize that I always had an excuse for Martha. I don't think I was ever afraid of her, but I didn't cross her either. She caused our mother pain by constantly arguing and fighting with her over everything. When Martha was a teenager, she would have roaring arguments with our mom and then come back to our rooms and tell me how funny it was to get Mom so stirred up. I felt sorry for Mom. She didn't have a chance with Martha. But I wouldn't stand up to her, because I knew she would then turn her torments on me.

"When Martha made up her mind to get something, she went after it and didn't stop until she had it. She wanted a yacht for her sixteenth birthday. Mom asked her what someone from the panhandle of Texas would do with a yacht. Our parents said no, that she could have a car of her choice, but not a yacht. Martha yelled and screamed, demanding her way. She wanted something special, something no one else would have. Everyone got a car for their sixteenth birthday, so she wanted something else. Our mom tried to reason with her, saying that yachts cost too much. Martha stood her ground and demanded that they use a portion of her inheritance that they give it to her early so she could enjoy what she wanted while she was young.

"Mom was horror-stricken, and it showed on her face. Before she could compose herself, Martha demanded to know what was wrong with her. I guess Mom couldn't tell Martha that she wouldn't get an inheritance of money. It was our father's opinion that only boys should inherit the assets of the family. He thought he was protecting his headstrong daughter from gold-diggers. She would only receive household items, jewels, anything that wasn't nailed down to the ranch.

"I remember our birthday, the day when we went to the DMV to get our licenses. I got mine, but Martha failed the driving portion. I drove all the time on the farm with Dad. She never got the chance to drive, except in driver's education, and she wouldn't get to drive with her class. She didn't want anyone to know that she didn't know how to do something. Power and control were very important to her.

"I got a car and drove to school the next day. She refused to go to school. She stayed home with our mom. When I got home that night, Mom was dead. She had a heart attack. Dad said that she had been arguing with Martha about the yacht again when she suddenly clutched her chest and couldn't breathe. She was foaming at the mouth when she collapsed. She had heart problems in her family, and she was overweight, so no one questioned it. But Bruce, I am beginning to wonder. Martha never shed a tear after Mom's death. She calmly told me how she watched our mom die. She said that Mom slobbered a little and then couldn't breathe. It was just like the dog. Martha confided in me that Mom told her she changed the will to give us equal shares of the estate when our parents died. I remember now she added, 'Mom shouldn't have done that.' Bruce what if she had something to do with our own mother's death?" Dad looks at me pleadingly.

"Dad I've never trusted Aunt Martha, but I never feared her until now. What you're saying makes sense. It explains a lot. I know this is hard, but keep going. Is there anything else that stands out in your memory of her?" I ask fearing that there is.

"After mom died my dad stayed gone more and more to buy cattle, leaving us with nannies. We were sixteen and resented having a babysitter. It wasn't long before we ran off every sitter he hired, and pretty soon Dad just let us govern ourselves. He still took me on our annual week-long get-away in the fall to the cave. Martha couldn't stand this. She wanted to know where we went and what we did. I was no match for Martha, and I knew it. I told her everything she wanted to know. I was always honest with her. I loved my sister and wanted desperately to make her happy." Dad continued. "When we turned twenty-one, our dad died in a freak car accident the day of our birthdays. Martha said that our mom told her we would gain half our inheritance when we turned twenty-one, and the rest upon their death. She didn't know until that day that Dad had changed his will after Mom died. He changed it back to me getting everything, but now it had stipulations.

Dad's will stated that I could not give her any money or property. If I tried to do this, then I would lose everything. Neither of us would receive anything, and all of the estate would go to various named charities. I always wondered about the car wreck. Dad was an excellent driver. He was careful. It just didn't make sense. There was no investigation into either of our parents' deaths, because Martha didn't want the publicity, and money can buy you a lot of privileges."

"Dad are you saying that you think she could've had something to do with grandma and granddad's death?" I ask shocked.

"Yes, I believe she is capable of anything. During Theresa's illness she didn't care about us. The fact that the deputy and his hit men knew exactly where the cave was and that we would be there further proves it. I can't explain away her actions any longer. Martha pressured me for years to put her in my will. I would always put her off. Now, I wonder if I signed our death warrant when I added her." Dad began to weep.

My heart goes out to Dad, but what he needs now is to visit with God. God is the only one able to give him the comfort and discernment he needs now.

Dad and I pray through the night for an end to our nightmare. I pray that God will place peace in our hearts.

The next morning we awaken to birds singing.

"Bruce I think when all of this is over we should go somewhere together. You can't come to Canadian with me and I can't be at the ranch with you, so what about Colorado?" Dad asks.

"Sure that would be great Dad. What do you have in mind?" I reply knowing dad is just trying to be positive for my sake.

"It is almost elk season, we can go to the cabin in Pagosa Springs. I think we need to use that old cabin again. It's been far too many years since we did anything together. I don't want to waste another minute." Dad says as his voice breaks.

"I'd love to do that. Can we spend the whole winter there?" I say feeling the same urgency to take advantage of life while we have it. I need this time with dad.

"I'm sure there will be some loose ends to tie up after all of this." Dad says, "I have an excellent group of people working for me. They know their jobs and I know they can run the company for the winter. I think it is time I take semi-retirement and maybe we will just spend the next couple of years together. We can live in a place that we both like. Let's start a new life?"

"Dad to be here with you is all I need." We stand and walk around the lake as we wait for the next call. It will tell us if we have this future together that we hope for or not.

We face our fears and neither one of us can settle in for the night. We are each deep in our own thoughts for a future together again. Time and trials has stolen more time than either one of us is willing to give away. From this moment on I know I will make sure my future has God and the people in my life that truly matters.

Lord I know you have brought us to this place in our lives for a reason. I pray. Please let that reason be so that we can heal and start a new life together. Keep me grounded in Your Word and Will Dear Lord.

Ted's next move is to call Washington. He's been owed a lot of favors over the past forty years, and he calls in most of them. The only people he puts on the case are those he would trust with his own life. They begin to gather the evidence needed to prove a conspiracy to commit murder.

Interlude

Canadian, Texas

Sheriff Taylor contacts two of his most trusted deputies and asks them to meet him. They go for a ride in a newly rented car. Sheriff Taylor tells them about his recent visit with an FBI agent. They make ready for a showdown. They are going to take back their office.

Chapter 13 - Peace

Ted calls the following night and says, "You can come home. I am coming after you personally. Tell me where you are, and I'll be right there," Ted says.

"We are at Lake Fryer on Wolf Creek," Dad tells him. "We'll be waiting. How will we know you?" We are still a little paranoid.

"I'm bringing Aunt Isabelle with me. We'll come in her Buick."

Ted hangs up, and we drop to our knees and silently pray prayers of thanksgiving. We pour our souls out to God and believe with all our hearts that God will give us peace. We look up from our prayers into each other's eyes and smile. Rising with peace in our hearts and our burdens lighter, we walk to the entrance of the lake, and to a bright future.

We take our money that Mrs. Felder gave us and walk to the restaurant at the lake on our way to the entrance. They are serving a buffet. The waitress comments on how we are eating like we haven't eaten in a month. We erupt into laughter releasing the last of the pent up tension.

We get to the entrance and ten minutes later a familiar older model Buick comes into view.

Mrs. Felder hugs us praising God. Ted Newton shakes our hands and we all get in the car. It is hard to believe we can go home, but neither one of us want to go to the ranch or the apartment. We ask Mrs. Felder if we can stay with her a night or two. She is so pleased and says yes.

"Mark your sister is the one behind all of the kidnapping and murder attempts." Ted says.

"Tell us what you found out." Dad replies.

"The Homeland Security team was bogus." Ted began. "Washington takes that seriously, and they are rounding up all kinds of people and putting them behind bars. Martha has been arrested on attempted murder charges. Get this—she wonders if she can room with her husband. We said no, of course. Still, when we thought it through, it sounded like a fair punishment to both of them."

"How could Aunt Martha have managed to do all of this?" I ask.

"Martha saved every dime you paid her to hire these thugs. She had sold everything in her home. She had received an advance on selling the house you bought her, but ran into a snag and couldn't complete the sale. The company owned the house. The thugs were to steal the will, deeds, and titles, so she would know for sure that she would inherit everything this time. She doctored the documents to show that, in the event of both yours and Bruce's death, she would inherit everything. She was afraid the original will might say something else and she wanted to be certain this time." Ted says.

"How did you manage to catch her?" Dad asks.

"Martha covered her tracks well. The only way we could prove anything was by that last name you gave us—Cindy Monroe. Martha hired Cindy after finding a photo of her that Bruce kept in a Fossil Watch tin box. Cindy didn't remember giving Bruce the photo, but she was game to do whatever Martha asked, because she would foot the bill for Cindy's drugs.

"Cindy was to get Bruce on drugs and then give him an overdose. She enjoyed the trips so much herself that she couldn't kill her only source of drugs. Martha staged a drug buy gone bad where Bruce was to be killed, but someone else came in his place to buy the drugs, and the killers didn't know that. This scared Cindy and she managed to get a rich tycoon to pay for everything and disappeared out of Martha's reach.

"Martha didn't figure we would ever find her, but we did, and Cindy admitted to everything. She said she really didn't want to hurt Bruce, so she would help us. She said it was Martha herself who paid her. When

Bruce was out of the way, Martha intended for you to have an accident, Mark. Cindy has told us every conversation she can remember. She may be a druggie but Cindy is smart. She taped all of her conversations with Martha." Ted replies.

"Did you find anything else?" Dad asks.

"Martha is a woman with lots of problems, though." Ted continues. "Martha confessed to killing your parents as well. It was as if she was playing poker, and she was laying down all the cards in her hand. She was talking like she'd won the card game. I'm so sorry Mark I know this is hard for you, but this information is what saved both of your lives."

"Mark you need to know that Sheriff Taylor and his deputies were working overtime on the case the whole time." Ted adds. "They put together the arson of the Theater and the hazardous tanker wreck that was only dry ice. They staged the accidents so that all law enforcement would be busy that night. The missing driver looked exactly like Deputy Lowe according to eye witness accounts. He wasn't a deputy at all. He was hired by Martha to kill you both. There was a woman with him named, Ann. We haven't found her yet, but the way everyone is spilling their guts to cut a deal, we should have her soon. They never gave up hope in finding you. They worked day and night to put together enough evidence to gain back control of their office so that they could make an arrest."

"Regain control of their office?" Dad asks. "Why weren't they in their office?"

"When Martha's team took over they gained control of everything, even the law. They took control under the impression that they were from Homeland Security. No one could prove otherwise." Ted continues. "Sheriff Taylor knew your families past and suspected Martha when she showed up at the Willis Cattle Company. She was in constant contact with the Homeland Security team and totally ignored Sheriff Taylor. He found out that she enlisted an architect to draw up plans for a mansion to be built on the existing ranch house site. The Sheriff knew then that he needed to work fast in order to save you."

"We will never be able to thank you, Mrs. Felder, and all of the law enforcement." I say.

"Isabelle I plan on paying you back your money with interest. It fed us when we needed it most. You will forever be a part of our family." Dad says.

Epilogue

Dad picks the baby up and carries him out to the patio. "When will dinner be ready? I'm starving," Renee, my beautiful wife comes around the corner with a salad. Behind her, my precious children follow, each carrying a portion of the meal.

"The steaks are coming off the grill now," I answer. "Have a seat. We're ready to eat." I turn to look at the ones I love, my beautiful wife, five kids, and Dad. We have two girls, Theresa and Isabelle, and three boys, Marcus, Ted and Richard; not that Richard Willis the accomplished actor of theater. I love it when Dad comes out to the ranch to spend some time and just hang out with the children. I understand, though, my Dad's need to work with the shelters and homeless. Dad and I could've chosen anywhere to live and we came home to the Canadian River Valley, with its voluminous canyons and spectacular vistas.

Each grandchild is truly a blessing from God. Dad and I both make sure that each child, boy or girl, has an abundance of attention and love from the father figures in their lives. Working with troubled families and homeless children brings Dad a special fulfillment.

We sit around the table and bow our heads. "Grandpa Mark, will you give thanks for the food?" seven-year-old Theresa asks.

Dad does. "Most gracious and heavenly Father," he prays, "we thank you for the abundance on and around this table. Continue to guide, guard, and protect us, helping us all to hear your voice and listen with our hearts. Amen."

I turn to Dad. "Theresa turns eight this fall," I remind him. "We are going to start our tradition of going to the cave. Do you want to join us?"

Dad beams. "Yes, I would love to come. Can you imagine? In another ten years, we'll have to find a bigger cave. I don't know if we can get everyone inside!"

Laughter fills the air like music on the wind, and the caliche dust on the mesas dances to the tune.

A Note from the Author

Did you enjoy, Not That Bruce Willis? Then you might like my next book on salvation. I draw the settings from the areas that I've lived near. Falcon Feather is an area in Blaine county in Oklahoma. The setting is real, but some features of the land have been moved to protect the area. This is a fictional piece of work, but historical facts are embedded within the story like they were in Not That Bruce Willis.

The Native Americans referred to in Falcon Feather were patterned after a group called the Fremont Indians. They lived on the western Colorado plateau and Utah. Known as part of the Four Corners Area Indians of the prehistoric era and their existence lasted about 900 years. Any resemblance to modern day tribes are purely coincidental.

Stop by my website: www.pamelajeanhoffman.com and check out the titles of other books written with the divine inspiration of my Lord.

Enjoy this excerpt from Falcon Feather;

A Story of Salvation

August 2011

Chapter 1

Cattails, Calamity, & Caves

Red-faced from my escape of the overgrown cattails, I think about last year when I was fourteen and wondering if I'd ever be as tall as the cattails. Well, I'm as tall as those darn exploding fuzz-bombs now. I used to think they looked like big cigars when I was a little boy. Now I'm certain they're the plant's first line of defense. No matter how gently I try to move them out of my way, they explode into an army of little fuzzy seeds that take flight, all of them heading for me like heat-seeking missiles. The fact that I need a haircut isn't to my benefit. I'm going to look like a porcupine with cotton balls all over my head. I hate it when my hair grows out a little and stands straight out in all directions, like a reddish-yellow halo. None of my brothers has coarse, straight hair. Mom calls the color strawberry blond, but I can't honestly think of a single guy who would describe his hair as strawberry blond.

"Achoo! Achoo! Achoo!" Sneezes always come in threes for me.

Not That Bruce Willis!

"Why do you always fish over there in the cattails?" Braden complains from across the pond. "You'll be sneezing all day and scaring off the fish!"

"I'll not be the one to chase the fish away. And for your information, I fish over here because this is where the spring is, *bro*," I call back, exaggerating the word bro to put him in his place. "The big fish like to cool down in that cool, fresh, natural spring water that constantly feeds into the pond. I've already caught five nice ones for supper. You should try it sometime, instead of lying over there, working on your tan."

"Five? We haven't even been here an hour yet. Coda, you're blowin' smoke!" Braden says, eyeing me to see if I'm joking.

I make my way from the west side of the pond to the north. The west side has a slightly steep, rocky wall, with cattails surrounding the southwest, west, and northwest side of the pond. The pond's dam is on the north—earth fills in the gap between my side of the canyon wall and Braden's east side. His is a gentle slope, leveling off with a grassy pasture on the top rim of the canyon. The earthen dam is wide enough to drive a car across.

"Well, I could've had five if I'd wanted," I say with conviction. "I guess the count is closer to one, but he's a big one!"

"I figured as much," Braden says and stretches out.

As I swat at the fuzz balls clinging to my sweaty bare skin, I wish I'd kept my shirt on, but it's so humid in the cattails I'd decided to lose the shirt. I notice how Braden's hair has grown out. His hair lays down when it gets a little length in it. He takes pride in how he looks, even when he's at the pond, fishing. He's clean-shaven, and his short, dark-brown hair is combed. Braden has a tan that gives him a healthy glow. I could stay outside every day and only get more freckles. I don't think I'll ever need to shave, because I have more pimples than whiskers.

What is up with all the pimples, God? You know how important it is for a guy to look his best as he enters high school. Sophomore year is coming up next month! How about You dry up these gross things once and for all? Maybe You could do that for my birthday in November.

"I'm going exploring downstream," I say, planning to follow the path along the northeast side of the dam next to the canyon wall. I run across the top of the dam where we've been fishing, and a cloud of fuzzy cattail puffs that have dislodged from my hair follow me like that dirt cloud of Pig-Pen's from the *Peanuts* cartoon strip. They hover, floating silently on the air, keeping pace with me as I sneeze all the way across the earthen embankment.

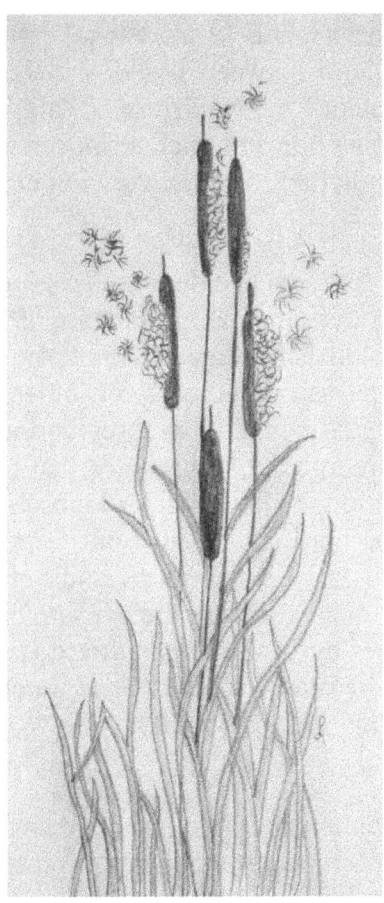

Not That Bruce Willis!

Between sneezes I call out, "I'll be back for lunch." I hike to the path leading over the backside. Over the years, the trees and brush have taken root on the dam, leaving only the one path to the bottom.

"Okay. I'll meet you here later. I want to fish," Braden replies, mumbling something under his breath and chuckling.

My older brother, Braden, is the best big brother. He may be four and a half years older than me, but he doesn't make me feel like a little kid. I have three younger brothers—Liam, Eli, and Fuller. Now, they're little kids! My two older sisters, Dulcie and Alexa, between Braden and me, add just enough cushion between us boys to keep the fights down. Sisters are good mediators, but Braden is still my favorite. He takes me fishing and hunting with him and tolerates my energy levels better than anyone else does. I'm hyperactive and very impulsive most of the time.

Our family farm is at the edge of Southard's United States Gypsum property. Dad works for them and does the training of new personnel. I find the history of the gypsum plant fascinating. I'm amazed that in the early years, they would hand dig and mine the gypsum from these canyons. There is also a salt creek just a few miles from here where salt was mined. The canyon's erosion exposes various layers of gypsum rock and red shale. George Southard mined that gypsum from 1905 to 1912. He then sold it to the United States Gypsum Corporation, which is our neighbor to the north and east of our farm. Our farm is rich in many ways, and the history surrounding it is just one of them—nomadic Indian tribes visited the land before the gypsum company. The natural spring here never goes dry, even in the driest seasons, so it would've been a good source of water for the Indians. Looking at the layers on the canyon wall, I think of the jawbreaker in my pocket. I pop it into my mouth and stroll along.

God, You put the earth together like one huge jawbreaker, didn't You? You wrapped layers of minerals and layers of rocks for us to find. What else have You hidden for me today?

My imagination runs wild as I make my way down the back of the pond's dam. I have a vivid imagination, and I can almost see the Indians of long ago, hunting deer nearby. I gaze at my surroundings as if I'm watching a live theater production. We've found several arrowheads

112

over the years around the spring. I wonder if I'll find any in the creek bottom today. My thoughts return to my own private outdoor theater. The Indians are dressed in buckskins, riding uniquely spotted paint ponies of chocolate, licorice, and cream. The ponies' colorful patches give definition to their muscles as they trot along. The buffalo, deer, and rabbits are in abundance, along with the grass and fresh water from the spring. My colorful imaginings help me to see the perfect place for a teepee encampment on the flat top of the canyon's eastern wall. I imagine the young boys and girls, helping the women as they set up their camp of teepees. All the adolescent boys and men would be getting their bows and arrows ready for the hunt. Their hunt tomorrow would be successful, because I'm sure there'll be deer just around this narrowing of the canyon.

I walk barefoot on native grass that is soggy from the water continually flowing from the overflow pipe in the dam. This allows the creek to have a constant flow of fresh water for the animals downstream. I turn the corner, and the canyon broadens, revealing a large area that's deep in the center and shallow along the edges. I duck, pretending an arrow has whizzed by my shoulder. I turn my head to see what my imaginary Indian companion is shooting at, and I see a real rabbit. After chasing the rabbit downstream, I see that this part of the ravine widens out and is thick with trees and brush near the canyon's walls. I must've run about fifteen yards from the dam. I stand now in knee-deep water and notice that it isn't moving much; in fact, it's pooling. I'm very observant that way. Mom says I am visually distracted by things.

God, I think You gave me a heightened awareness of Your world. The reason I jump from one thing to another isn't because I have ADD; it's because You also gave me an urgency to experience everything You've made.

I look around, wondering why the water has stopped flowing. The pool gets increasingly deeper for the next twenty-five yards, so I move to a ledge above the water level, and I find the answer. A beaver has set up residence on the creek. I look around and, not seeing the rodent, I confidently give him fair warning, calling out in a commanding voice, "Grandma says you're going to have to go, Mr. Beaver. You tried this a few years ago, and Grandma took care of you. Well, Grandma's not here, but Coda, defender of the burr oaks, is here!" I beat my bare chest for good measure and stand tall in my cut-off jean shorts. A few fuzz balls dislodge from my bare skin, though others remain in my hair as I look at my reflection in the still water.

Hearing no response, I move closer and think that the beaver's amazing engineering talents must definitely be God-given. By the size of the dam and lodge, I guess there are probably at least two beavers living here. Beavers mate for life, and so up to two litters could be living with their parents, based on the size of the beaver lodge.

I say loudly, "Mr. and Mrs. Beaver, I hope you don't think that you are like a cousin or anything to me, just because you have a dad, mom, and kids. You beavers have killed the burr oaks!" They've chewed all the way around the tree trunks. Grandma told me the summer before she died that one day, the burr oaks would be completely wiped out of this area. Even now, the burr oaks are nearly all gone. "Sorry, Mr. Beaver," I call out, "but you're going to have to move." Dad has said if the beaver pond backs up to the bottom of my pond's dam, it'll weaken it, causing my dam to give way, and that's another reason Grandma sent the beavers packing. I raise my voice one more time, shouting, "You're not going to wreck my dam!" I walk next to the canyon wall and come to the beaver's dam. It stretches from one side of the canyon's wall to the other, making a fairly wide pond. I read a book on beavers when I was little and remember that it takes a half-mile of habitat to support one family. I try to stand on the shale edge of the pond and pull the limbs from the dam. The sheer cliff wall behind me makes it difficult to bend over. I have to be careful not to land headfirst in the water.

Don't laugh, God. I know You have a sense of humor. I dare You to try it—stand with Your back to a wall and then bend over and pick up something from the floor … or a cloud … in front of You. See? I told You. I imagine God is laughing.

I look around but don't see the beavers. I wade in about chest high and begin tearing the logs, limb by limb, from the dam. The water begins to flow over the top, slowly at first, and then it picks up speed. That is when it happens.

Pow! Pow! Pow!

114

Vibrations ripple across the water where the bullets must've hit. I whirl around, searching the canyon walls for the hunter, but I remember that July is not hunting season. Is someone shooting at me? I don't think imaginary Indians can come to life.

"Braden! Did you hear that?" I scream. And then thinking that I sound like a girl, I shout again, lowering my voice this time, "Braden!"

Oo! Oo! Oo! A mournful seal-like barking is right behind me. Is that an Indian calling to his buddy? Am I surrounded? Spinning in the now waist-deep water, I spot him. He's large; he's brown with slick, dark hair and beady eyes, black as coal, glaring at me. The top of his head and his eyes are all that's above the water. Volumes are spoken in those few seconds between me and Mr. Beaver. I can almost hear him say,

Not That Bruce Willis!

"How dare you destroy my home? The missus and I just finished the remodeling." He'd speak in beaver language, of course—a language in which I am fluent, by the way.

The "gunshots" now made sense—it was the beaver, slapping his powerful flat tail on the water, sounding the alarm for the other beavers. *Other beavers!* I look left, right, and behind me as I back toward the canyon wall and the path leading back to Braden. Mr. Beaver moves closer. He swims effortlessly. I, on the other hand, can't seem to move where I want to go. The current is pulling me.

"Beaver! Braden, a beaver is after me! Help me!" I scream.

The hair on the back of my neck stands up, and I feel like there is something or someone right behind me. Goose bumps begin to pop up on my skin. The expression "My hair stood up on end" is literally true. As the hair stands up, it pulls the skin slightly, making goose bumps. I try to climb out of the water, but I seem to panic a little as I feel pokes and scratches on my legs and feet. I mean, it could be the claws of a mega-beaver or a bunch of baby beavers! I look back … and the beaver is submerged. He's under the water, sneaking up on me. I know he is!

"Help me!" I sound like a girl again, and I don't even care.

The logs I'd dislodged let the water begin to spill over the top of the dam, and it's moving more limbs. My long, boney legs get tangled in the debris underwater, and I go under. Spitting and sputtering, I resurface and find I'm floating with the current of rushing water, closer to the dam and the family's lodge home.

"Oh no!" I scream.

It's the last place I want to be, so I grab a branch that's hanging over the water's edge. It's too small to hold my weight and breaks, sending me into the water again. Squealing, I realize the water is not over my head; I can stand up at any time. Gee whiz, I've got to get a grip on myself and get out of here. The logs roll and spin, flipping me flat on my back for a third time. Lying on the bottom of the now-drained pond, I tilt my head backwards and peer over the top of my forehead. The scene is upside down, but I see not one but two large, smiling beavers lumbering toward me.

"Braden!" I scream again.

They look happy—no, angry! Those big orange tusk-like teeth are not smiling; they are ready to chew me up and spit me out! I'm done for; I know it! I manage to get upright one more time. Most of the water is going down the creek bed, leaving the pond looking kind of small now. I glance over my shoulder, and the beavers are halfway across the dry pond, still coming toward me. My only chance of survival is to leap out of the water and onto the shale shelf, just above where the pond used to be. I make it and turn to see one beaver lumbering up the side of the damp pond; the other is blocking my getaway, should I try to go downhill. Mr. Beaver takes his time in toying with me, like a cat would do with a mouse—trapping it and then letting it go, only to trap it again. I can't use the path in either direction. Downstream is Mrs. Beaver, and upstream are thickets of thorny foliage. Mr. Beaver continues toward me. The only way to save myself is to climb the wall. I move closer and find a couple of rocks to hold on to and a couple of rocks to step upon. Slowly, I climb higher and higher. I'm about three feet off of the ground when I feel his whiskers brush the calf of my leg.

Someone not as familiar with the wild as I am might think it was only the leaves of the bush, but the outdoorsman that I am, I know the difference. I'm so sure it's a beaver. I can see in my mind those enormous orange tusk-like teeth biting down on the soft tissue of the back of my leg. Up, up I climb! Nothing like an image like that to get a person motivated. When I'm about six feet off the ground, the rocks I'm using as handholds give way—and down I come, screaming like a girl again. I'll be glad when my voice decides to land an octave lower. Before I hit the ground, my fall is broken by the two-inch thorns of the thicket, which first become entangled in my cut-off jean shorts and then hold me off of the ground by grabbing me and thrusting deeply into my skin. I'm hanging upside down by my pants and skin. I'm wedged between the wall of the canyon and a bunch of thorny bushes! At least my face is toward the cliff wall and not toward the thorns, even if I did scrape it in a place or two. It's important to always find the positive in life. I try to free myself, but I'm stuck tight, and with each movement, the thorns rip my flesh. I wonder if my long toes look like tender burr oak limbs to a beaver. Why do I think of such horrors?

"Help me, Braden! Help!" I scream as loudly as I can.

And I hear Braden mocking me. *"Help me, Braden! Help!"*

How dare he make fun! I call again, "Braden, I'm serious!"

"Braden, I'm serious!"

What in the world is going on? That's not like him? Then I have an idea, so I test my theory. "Hello!"

"Hello!"

Just as I thought: it's an echo, and it's coming from the wall. I see a crack running through the layer of rock and an opening at the bottom of the wall. There must be a cave. How exciting! I can't wait to tell Braden. I feel cool air on my face, and the air continues to move over my face like a steady breeze. This is definitely a cave, and one with another opening somewhere, by the feel of this draft of air.

"Coda, how in blazes did you get back there?" Braden asks. He begins to pick at and pull the thorns bushes back so he can reach me.

"Braden, I found a cave, I think," I say with excitement.

"Coda, you have been screaming bloody murder, like you were being mauled by bears or something. I nearly broke my neck, running down here just to see a cave—not even a cave; it's a crack in the wall!" Braden pokes himself with a thorn while pulling one out of me. He seems mad, so I decide I'd better tell the whole story. The sweat on his athletic body shows the exertion from his run down the dam and through the humidity of the canyon. His damp face scowls, and his hazel eyes snap from the green of the leaves to the blue of the sky.

"There was a beaver after me, and I fell in here when I tried to climb up the wall," I explain. "Watch your back, Braden. That beaver is stealth-like. There're two of them, but the male is the one after me. They may look slow, but they can put on a move when they want. I'm sure some of these scratches are from his huge claws. You should see his teeth! Look around to see if he's gone, because if he isn't, you might not fare as well as I have. Find something to protect yourself."

"The only thing I see is a skinny little brother hanging upside down, tangled up in a thorn bush, wedged next to a rock face wall. You don't look like you're faring very well yourself. What did you do to the beaver anyway?" Braden asks as he looks around. Then he tries to free me, while not slicing himself in the process. Poking himself, he yells, "Ouch!"

"I was tearing down his dam so he'd move. Grandma said they love to eat burr oaks and that we don't have many left, that those trees are almost extinct," I say, hearing my echo.

"Those trees are almost extinct."

"Do you hear that echo?" I ask. "I bet there's a big cave. We should explore it. I feel a cool breeze coming out of this crack. There must be another opening somewhere for the air to draw through here. Wasn't it lucky of me to fall right here, with my face smashed up to the wall? Just think—I might've missed discovering this cave if this hadn't happened." I prattle on, realizing that when my attention goes skittering across time like this, it makes me sound unfocused.

"Ouch!" Braden yells again when my twisting to see the cave causes him to get poked. "Coda, stay still and tell me about the beaver!" Braden shouts. He is more than a little upset with those thorns, I'm sure. They're a pain.

"He's big, furry, and mean," I respond.

"I'm going up to the pickup and get a hatchet and a shovel," Braden says angrily.

"That's a good idea. Get that big one with the hatchet first. Then what? Are you going to bury him with the shovel?" I ask, realizing as I finish my thought that it doesn't make much sense and that Braden always makes sense. Braden doesn't answer. "Don't leave me. Where's that beaver? Look for that beaver first. Do you see him?" I plead, totally serious this time. I try to turn my head to look at the canyon and end up poking my face with thorns. My only view is of this crack in the wall.

"You stay right there," Braden laughs. I can't believe he's laughing! "I'll be back. This is the first time all day that I'll know for sure where to find you and that you won't be getting into trouble while I'm gone. I may get a little fishing in after all." He continues to cackle as he walks up the dam ever so slowly.

"Braden, don't joke! Where's the beaver?" I exclaim. "It's not nice to torment a guy when he's down! I mean up … or upside down! Oh! You know what I mean!"

"It may take me an hour or two to find that hatchet and shovel," he calls from the path leading to the dam.

www.ingramcontent.com/pod-product-compliance
Lightning Source LLC
Chambersburg PA
CBHW051259170626
46809CB00004B/1716